The Infamous Rosalie

Évelyne Trouillot

The Infamous Rosalie

{ Rosalie l'Infâme }

Translated by M. A. Salvodon
Foreword by Edwidge Danticat

UNIVERSITY OF NEBRASKA PRESS

LINCOLN & LONDON

Cet ouvrage a bénéficié du soutien
des Programmes d'aide à la publication
de l'Institut Français.

This work, published as part of a program
of aid for publication, received support
from the Institut Français.

Publication of this book was assisted
by a grant from the
National Endowment for the Arts.

ART WORKS.
arts.gov

Library of Congress
Cataloging-in-Publication Data
Trouillot, Evelyne, 1954–
[Rosalie l'infâme. English]
The infamous Rosalie = : Rosalie l'Infâme
/ Évelyne Trouillot; Translated by M. A.
Salvodon; Foreword by Edwidge Danticat.
pages cm
Originally published: Paris: Éditions
Dapper, 2003.
ISBN 978-0-8032-4026-1 (pbk.: alk. paper)
I. Title.
PQ2680.R656R6713 2013
843'.914—dc23   2013006175

Set in Garamond Premier Pro by
Laura Wellington. Designed by A Shahan.

In memory of my uncle, Hénock Trouillot,
historian and scholar, whose writings
on everyday life in Saint-Domingue were
an immense help to me . . .

Foreword

EDWIDGE DANTICAT

History is often written by victors. Perhaps this is why, when discussing Haitian history, we tend to linger more on the battles we've won rather than the ones we lost, the ones where we lost our people, our humanity, ourselves.

Everyone who cares to know is aware that Haiti was the first black republic in the Western Hemisphere, the first place in the world where slaves defeated their masters and started their own nation. However, few people know what it meant for these eventual victors, or their parents and grandparents, to have survived the specific route of the Middle Passage that led to what was once Ayiti, Quisqueya, and which would later became Hispaniola and Saint-Domingue and finally Haiti.

The *Code noir*, that brutal decree passed in 1685 by France's Louis XIV to terrorize those who were in bondage in France's colonies, gives us some idea what life was like for a slave; that and the journals, wills, and sale records of colonists and slave masters. Yet we rarely hear—even in fiction—from ordinary people, such as Lisette, the narrator of this book, about their daily activities, their few joys, and their constant agonies and pain.

The Infamous Rosalie changes that. Embracing a singular and direct, fact-inspired narrative, it shows the individual experiences of ordinary women and men (and even some famous ones) and the scars they bear from the horrors of a then not-so-distant Middle Passage as well as from slavery. One can never know what it is like to make certain choices unless one finds oneself in that very same position under the very same circumstances. This is perhaps why we are not always comfortable discussing situations like the ones so masterfully portrayed in this book. The wounds, though inflicted long ago, are still there. We are still mothers. We are still daughters. We are still men. We are still women. We are still human, no matter how much some would want this not to be true.

In 2005 I had the pleasure of interviewing Évelyne Trouillot for *BOMB* magazine. During a bicentennial conference hosted by the University of the West Indies at its Saint Augustine campus in Trinidad, I heard her talk about how Haitian history is often discussed only in terms of the triumphs of the Haitian Revolution in 1804 and how little attention is paid to what came before that revolution: the pre-Columbian indigenous period, the post-Columbian genocides, the slave trade and colonization period. In our interview I asked her why she thought that was.

"The emphasis was always put on the great figures, the heroes," she said, "and not on the mass of enslaved and of newly freed slaves. While writing *Rosalie l'Infâme*, I learned about the struggles of the enslaved women, men, and children in their daily lives; their struggles to maintain their dignity. And I truly believe that if the slaves had not fought for their dignity, if they had not managed to maintain some dignity amid the most inhuman system, the Haitian Revolution would not have been possible. While doing my research for writing *Rosalie*, I could empathize with them because finally I saw them as human beings and not as an anonymous mass of victims of slavery."

I am so glad to see Évelyne Trouillot's powerful novel translated into English by the equally talented Marjorie Salvodon. Now a whole new group of readers can participate in this growing shattering of silences around these increasingly less anonymous voices of the ultimate *victors* over slavery.

Acknowledgments

First and foremost, I would like to thank Évelyne Trouillot for writing a novel that highlights the significant role of the women who resisted slavery in eighteenth-century Saint-Domingue and for answering all my questions with grace, intelligence, and promptness.

I am thankful for the invaluable comments made by the anonymous readers at the University of Nebraska Press on the first draft of the manuscript and for the meticulous and insightful review of successive drafts of this translation by Laura Pirott-Quintero, Michael Reder, and Faith Smith. I appreciate the travel grant I received from Suffolk University's Faculty Development Committee, which enabled me to travel to Haiti in 2011, and thank the College of Arts and Sciences Dean's Office, whose research funds enabled Sandy Germain to work on this project as my research assistant.

As always, the support of my family and friends in Haiti, France, and the United States inspires me to be attentive to words and their various contexts, whether in English, French, Spanish, or Haitian. I want to extend a special thank-you to Mark Schafer for his generosity, his skills as a wordsmith, and his thorough review of a previous draft of this translation. May we continue to swim together in the sea of languages!

The Infamous Rosalie

I WEAVE THROUGH THE MAZE OF paths between the shacks, taking care to go the back way, avoiding the one window through which I can glimpse the dark, damp rooms inside the house. My blue serge skirt swirls around my legs, and I hold it up with one hand to keep it out of the puddles from yesterday's rain. I run, ignoring the occasional scolding looks and grumblings that follow me, responding to well-meaning advice with a flick of my hand.

"Hurry up, Lisette, or you'll be in trouble with your mistress!"

"The food is ready, Lisette. What are you doing out here?"

My legs seem possessed by an incredible speed, never hesitating as they follow the path between the shacks without faltering—as if they were skimming the surface of the stones, raising the fine dust brightened by the noonday sun. I don't see anything as I run. The screams of Paladin's children as their father was burned at the stake on the Beauplan plantation still resound beneath my skin. The master had commanded all Negroes to bring something to stoke the fire with and to watch the spectacle. Slipping into the crowd, I saw Paladin's two daughters, Lolotte and Marinette, watching their father stamp his feet and shriek.

"Vile, godless scoundrel, unworthy of being counted among men, crueler than the wild beasts . . .

"For attempting to murder your fellow men and employing underhanded and shameful means to destroy your master's house and endanger the goods bestowed upon him by divine Providence, the atrocity of your crime merits death and every kind of torment. But because the Holy Church does not refuse he who is willing to repent and rectify his errant ways . . ."

Beauplan had prepared things well. The beadle was there, prayer book in hand, to lend a sacrosanct atmosphere to the execution. The prayer damning the poisoners rose above the screams of the two girls, making the scene unreal. Everyone was sweating, and I realize I'd been balancing on the tips of my toes when the woman next to me punched me in the ribs. My tears began to flow, but I continued watching the madness of the flames in spite of myself. The charred skin stuck to my pupils, darkening the depths of my soul. Before my eyes a human body turned to ashes.

"Lisette, we're waiting for you in the big house. Where did you go?"

I inhabit the final spasms of Paladin, whose face, before it was turned into a mask of horror by the sizzling stake, I'm unable to reconstruct. I inhabit the fingers of this same man as he plucks the strings of his *banza* on a night of calendas, with the music enchanting us. I inhabit the streaks that disfigure him, from his shoulder to his ribs, long tracks of raised welts swollen with memories of the hot branding irons, and their imprints, of belonging and suffering. I inhabit the *chica*, dancing under the bower, prisoner of the advancing hour and the stars that herald the end of our illusory freedom. I am the wind, tethered to the ground.

I speed past Ma Victor's shack, turn left at Mam'zelle Jeanne's shack, then run all the way to the big house. I reach the back door just as Ma Augustine is coming out. She looks exasperated.

"At last, Lisette! Where have you been? Madame is about to sit down to eat."

"I'm coming. I'm coming."

I quickly rinse my face, wash my hands and feet, shake out my skirt, and smooth my wrinkled blouse. Grumbling the whole time, Ma Victor pours sauces into small earthenware bowls. Ma Augustine, my godmother, hangs a clean apron around my neck, and I walk into the dining room ahead of her. A minute later my mistress, Madame Clémentine Fayot, enters the room in a swish of silk and lace.

I've grown skilled in the art of averting my eyes. As I peek through the lace my mistress wears around her wrists, neck, skirts, and slips, I cast a glance, half-complicit, half-suspicious, at Gracieuse—the cocotte, who hopes that the favors she provides her masters will one day gain her her freedom. Cocotte, dear cocotte, say my laughing eyes as my body plays out this charade, this servile comedy, trying to avoid any trouble that my excessive absence may have provoked; my arms dangle innocently at my hips, my neck grows shorter, and my buttocks contract. Gracieuse isn't fooled by my submissive posture. Like a true Congo woman, she sways her hips as she follows her mistress; her smile exposes my subterfuge.

"Where did you go, you little stupid thing, that your

breath stinks of hate? Won't you ever understand that the sun, even when it sets on the sea, never gets wet?"

Gracieuse carries the bamboo fan regally. Every movement of her hand transmits a message full of wet kisses, sweet and languorous caresses, forbidden whisperings, delectable pleasures. Madame lets herself fall voluptuously into her chair, while Monsieur seems unable to take his eyes off Gracieuse's arms; her own eyes are half-shut. Hypnotized by her suggestive, lascivious gestures, the slow, smooth, to-and-fro of the fan, and her heavy, coaxing eyes, my masters seem uninterested in me for the moment.

"Don't meddle in the business of the master and his cocotte. Things aren't as simple as you think." That's what Augustine often says when I complain about the privileges Gracieuse enjoys, especially ever since the departure of Mademoiselle Sarah, the master and mistress's daughter.

"I'm Sarah's Negress," I said one day long ago, when Grandma Charlotte was still alive. Back in our shack, she slapped me in the face. "I don't want you ever to think that thought again, Lisette. Arada women belong to no one."

I have a long history with beatings, enough to know them well and to mistrust them. Even in my privileged position working for Mademoiselle Sarah, I was never protected. Sarah herself, despite having been forbidden from hitting me, couldn't always control herself and sometimes did. Or she would invent stories of broken toys, beheaded dolls, or soiled slips to wield the power she held. A young Creole girl born to well-heeled planters, she had tutors, dance and music instructors, and regularly received sweetmeats from France. Ten, twenty, even fifty lashes for the worse offenses—the whip and I share a long history of blows and evasions, of crashes and missed encounters. From tears to screams, from moans to silences, I have mastered the entire expressive range of my voice to spare my skin. The whip's traces aren't visible: they've lodged in the hollow of my hand, and I feel as if my guts are dragging under my feet, though no one can see them. But on that long ago day, when Grandma Charlotte was still alive, the slap of her hand left its mark on my cheek. It gathered the pitfalls of my hidden desperation: the scattered bits and pieces of shame, the urge to express my anger and the morsels of my tears and my betrayal, and it wove them all together in a single brusque movement more powerful than the whip. I still feel the sharp stinging sound coursing through me, her disdain for my unease and fear, her lack of pity for my bowing and scraping. I rest on the wings of that gesture whenever my knees refuse to bend to refresh my pupils in the darkness of their truth.

I begin to serve the meal. First, the aperitif, which must be removed from the small, locked cabinet. Then I spoon a bit of each dish on the plate of Ma Victor's great-niece, Manon. Standing next to the large mahogany dresser, a few steps away from my mistress, Manon tastes every dish at every meal. When it seems like she's survived the meal, I serve Monsieur and Madame and their guests, if there are any. Without saying a word, with a curtsy befitting her eight years, the young girl then joins the other slaves in the kitchen.

We are in the midst of a reign of terror that is convulsing the northern part of the Big Island. Blacks and whites, slaves and masters alike, everybody trembles with fear, barely daring to touch the food they are served. Men spy on their women and mistresses. Mothers look suspiciously at their lovers and neighbors. The dreaded fear of poison has invaded every residence, breeding utter confusion and mistrust. From large to small shacks, from one alley to the next, everyone distrusts everyone else. A month doesn't go by without four or five men or women being burned, accused of having poisoned Negroes or whites. Paladin is just one more entry on a long list of names.

For a while now that's all the Fayots talk about at the dinner table. The guests seem to be in a competition to tell stories of Negro poisoners, of a valet who killed his longtime protector, of a mulatto woman who got rid of her master to obtain the freedom he had promised her more quickly, of slaves killing themselves to escape slavery. The colonists are fascinated by these incidents, which they repeat to one another in whispers. They lower their voices noticeably every time Rose-Marie, broom or rag in hand, walks down the corridor. They look up with irritation whenever Florville comes to bother the master for this or that emergency, but they speak freely in front of me and Gracieuse, Madame's cocotte. Am I not Lisette, granddaughter of Charlotte, an Arada woman who was the house cook until she died of smallpox? Ma Augustine had always been responsible for the housekeeping, supervising Rose-Marie and the slave children. Even though Ma Victor took Grandma Charlotte's place, the masters don't trust her entirely. Master Fayot calculated that she'd think twice before risking the life of her great-niece, even if she wanted to poison the Fayot family. That's why Manon eats before the masters do every day. I wonder if she understands that on any given day a mouthful could cause her great suffering and death. Yet Manon is the daughter of Franchette, who was Madame's cocotte for years, before Gracieuse. Madame Fayot always said that with Franchette's fingers combing their hair, she and her daughter were sure to be among the most elegantly dressed women in town. Franchette died in labor, and since then Ma Victor has taken care of the child. Ma Augustine was not surprised by Madame's actions: "Believe me, Lisette, don't try to understand these Creole women. They caress you in the morning and have you whipped at night."

Dwelling within me is my true vision, the one that refuses all servility, that glides over the damask tablecloth, Madame's gold jewelry, the bottles of wine picked off crates just unloaded from Bordeaux, the patios filled with flowers, the clipped hedges that were my hiding place and refuge since Grandma Charlotte's time, the broad roads, the fields of sugarcane, the bare-chested Negroes in short britches, the workrooms, the Negroes' gardens that extended all the way to the mountains—all the way to the hills that surround us, so close, so far. My movements are mechanical: I set the dishes Ma Augustine hands me on the table, I remove the empty plates, I fill the empty glasses. I barely eat, so I can be free during the nap my master and mistress take. The cocotte will keep them company. The departure of Mademoiselle Sarah gave me greater freedom of movement, since the master and mistress only think of me at mealtimes, when the heat is oppressive, or when company arrives and there are large dinners followed by dances, which the mistress loves to organize. As long as there are enough maids to slap around, the master and mistress don't pay attention to every little thing we do! I scrub the saucepans, the *couis*, the calabashes Jeannine rinses with water then turns over to dry in the basket. As the oldest of the slaves working as maids in the house, Ma Augustine supervises cleaning and cooking. She doesn't let me leave until I've finished my chores, and honestly, it never would have occurred to me to do that. The only thing that betrays my haste to leave is the speed and dexterity of my hands.

"Don't be too eager to glimpse the sun's rays, my child. The sun can also announce that rain is on the way."

No, I won't question your wise words, Ma Augustine. There are moments when life doesn't let patience or reason interfere but swirls around the pebbles on life's road, the bee's sting and the foolishness of the wind.

"Hey Lisette!" Fontilus, the son of Gentilus the baker, calls to me as I pass by him in a flash. "Did you poison anyone today? Can we eat now?"

I shoot back my answer in the same mocking tone, without even turning to look at him.

"Watch out, Fontilus! On the Lalanne plantation the baker was accused of poisoning the flour. Tell your father to watch out."

"Stop it, you two," Ma Victor orders. She's sitting in front of a basket full of unshelled peas, with Manon beside her. "It's no joke."

Fontilus and I both laugh with the same, slightly hopeless delirium, as I keep going, feeling his gaze lingering on my buttocks.

"You're tall and have the large buttocks of women of our race," Ma Augustine told me. "You're as beautiful as your great-aunt Brigitte." She says I'm a Creole, born on the Big Island, and that I carry within me all the gestures of the Arada race, the race of my mother. Fontilus says that the tinge of yellow in my skin reminds him of nearly ripe mangoes, which explains why I have such a wholesome character. "You're not ripe yet," he tells me. Fontilus teases me to no end, but one day I overhear him saying that his thighs dance the *chica* with delight when he sees me pass by.

Ma Victor, always ready to speak her mind on the subject of Negroes, states that Congo men like Fontilus have two faults: they think with that thing between their legs, and they get way too much pleasure from drinking brandy and fighting. Arada women, on the other hand, often have the power to predict the future.

Regarding the future, I just want to be certain of my next meeting with Vincent. I stay away from the workrooms, the damp-walled *ajoupas** belonging to the field slaves, and the smell of droppings from men and animals that clings to the trees and clouds. I take off, imitating the movement of leaves bursting with nostalgia and exuberance, like despairing petals. My braids swell under the weight of the raindrops that run down my back. When the rain stops, I notice I've been crying for a while, that my eyelids—possessed by the image of the burning stake—counter my good-natured thoughts.

Suddenly Vincent is standing there, solid and sure, full of the brown, rocky earth in which I bury my tears. Everything comes out: the flames, the screams, the fear, the anguish, the

* Hastily assembled, tall huts covered with leaves.

shame, the indignation, the anger and the rage. I let my fingers reacquaint themselves with his arms—those mysterious lianas, strengthened by every marking and brand on his chest. Beneath the burns he took on of his own volition, I rediscover again the stamp of the inhuman trade, marking much more than his skin. I greet them again. I run my fingers and lips over his skin for a long time, let my tongue find refuge there, seeking tenderness and freedom. Vincent's large hands take stock of the different parts of my body as well, rediscovering my breath, my nightmares, my braids pinned against my ears, my doubts, my hips, my breasts.

"Where is your *garde-corps*,* Lisette?"

Ma Augustine had made me take off the talisman I always wore, the one Grandma Charlotte gave me. I would wear it inside my blouse, against my chest. It was a way to remember Grandma Charlotte and the mother I never knew.

Ma Augustine commanded, "Burn it, hide it far from here, throw it in the river, but don't have it on you. They hang people for less than that. Negroes are forbidden from wearing these talismans."

As I made my way toward the rear of the shack I shared with her, Ma Augustine added, "Get rid of your aunt Brigitte's cord as well."

"Why?" I stuttered, but my godmother's inscrutable face silenced my protests.

That day I took the piece of cord with its many knots that had belonged to my great-aunt Brigitte, Charlotte's

* The *garde-corps* was a kind of talisman worn by rebellious slaves that was said to make them invulnerable to firearms and release them from the fear of whites.

sister, from the calabash where I kept my *rassade* drop earrings, my burned spelling book, the piece of white lace I had taken from one of Mademoiselle Sarah's blouses, and the small golden jewel I have no right to wear. I removed my talisman made of rooster feathers, sand from an hourglass, and leather and went to place my treasure at the very top of the mango tree, behind the shacks, deep in a hollow I'd discovered long ago. I couldn't bring myself to destroy them. I already felt too vulnerable, as if an important part of me had been torn away. Yet it never occurred to me to disobey Ma Augustine.

"I'm leaving you in your godmother's care," Grandma Charlotte had told me before she died. "She's a ship sister, an Arada woman like us. She knew your great-aunt Brigitte well."

The name of my great-aunt is itself a talisman, as powerful as the one she gave me. I hang onto it in moments of despair, when I'm about to succumb to my sinking morale.

"Brigitte was so beautiful and still young when I knew her," Ma Augustine had told me. "Her two sons died trying to protect her. Two young boys killed in front of their mother as well as their aunt Charlotte, your grandmother. But Brigitte always smiled when she spoke of them, for she could not have borne to see them enslaved. 'Better dead than slaves,' she would often say. And her voice, so proud, gave us back our strength and dignity."

"We must trust both grandmas," Vincent says, accepting Ma Augustine's decision immediately, without ever having met her. "They know many things."

Until those happy moments when we're together again, the violence and horror trouble us deeply. Vincent talks about the recent arrival of slave ships, the new Maroons who have escaped and joined his group, the raids by the constabulary, now more determined than ever to capture them, the Maroons' visits to the plantations to get two Nago women who wanted to join their men, the loss of three companions, dismembered after being captured. Only my fingers show the fear I feel for my man: they tremble on his shoulders, on his hair tied back in a ponytail that brushes his neck, in his coarse and abundant beard. I shudder, but I silence my fears and tell him about the fear of poison that has traveled the length and breadth of the plantations, the measures taken by the colonists, the men and women who have been tortured and burned.

His face tenses slightly, but his voice doesn't waver. "The whites don't seem to understand that the danger will take different paths but that each path will intersect with the others in good time."

We're asleep under the shade of a large poisonwood tree, from which Vincent can survey the surrounding area. He places his hand on my sex and holds it there soft and still, like a serene, sure comfort. I fall asleep amid the beauty of this land that seems to bear the mark of our pain—Creoles, Aradas, Congos, Nagos, Ibos, newly arrived Negroes, forever *bossales*,* confronting our chains. In my sleep I struggle against miasmas and stagnant waters, barracoons and the steerage of ships, the growl of dogs, bodies too hot and damp, the sound of bludgeons.

Vincent's mischievous finger wakes me, and soon we are

---

* Slaves who had recently arrived in the colony, as opposed to "Creoles," who were men and women born in the colony, whether of African or European heritage.

swept up in a tumult of movement and maddening words. Our laughter stops abruptly as we let our passion consume our hidden fear and anguish.

"You have to go back, Lisette."

"Yes, I know. Actually, I promised Michaud I'd stop by and see him this afternoon."

As usual, Vincent stands to watch me leave. I almost always look over my shoulders at the last mountain slope where the hills hide him from me completely, as if once again he's disappeared into the bark of a tree or the bend of a stone wall. When will I see him again? When will I get the next sign telling me whether it will be in one day, three weeks, or two months? I ask the Good Lord to protect him. Luckily, my man was able to keep his talismans and his knife. I don't dare think about what would happen to him if he were captured—or rather, I imagine all too well the atrocities to which he would be subjected. Maroons have severed legs and ears, burned genitals, chained feet; they are cast aside to be sold with missing body parts, maimed and half-dead, when they're not devoured by mastiffs.

Sometimes I tell myself that it's too risky for Vincent to come see me, even if the Fayot plantation is miles away and no one knows about us. But I'm never able to bring up my reservations when I see him. From that moment on, all of my senses are focused on endlessly multiplying the movement of his hands, the sounds of his desire, the power of his pleasure, the tenderness of his eyes, the tickle of his beard on my chest, the frenzy of his sex against mine.

"I need you," he told me one day when my eyes were more bewildered than usual. His former master had just posted a new broadside calling for his capture.

Please return Vincent, a runaway slave known as The Fearless One, a Nago Negro, age approximately twenty-four years, novice coachman, good knowledge of French, sometimes passes for a free man, escaped nine years ago.

"May your fear be as strong as your anger, my love. You and freedom both relish the rising sun and mother's milk. Your love makes me want to look at the sky."

My feet brought me home just as swiftly. Before reaching the workrooms, I turn right and stop when I come to a small shack in the middle of a yard. I always slow down when I get here, as if remembering the slaves discarded by the master weighs down my every step. All the people who can no longer work: Désirée, a sixty-year-old Mina Negress who walks with difficulty because of the burns on her legs and thighs; Pierrot, a Congo Negro, who had pox three years ago and now carries his distress on his ravaged face; Clarens, Rosalie's baby, who was born hunchback and is barely learning to walk; Charlot, a short, newly arrived Negro who was already disabled when he got off the boat and was discarded from the beginning, who cultivates the vegetable garden with the help of Victor, Ma Victor's oldest son—Charlot, who must be about sixteen but acts like a child. And of course, Michaud the former overseer, who lost his arm as a result of an accident. They all come running over when they see me. It's always like this when someone visits these neglected people. I give the children, including Victor, macaroons that I took from the small cupboard. For the others I've brought boiled ripe bananas; they are cold and soft but sweet. Michaud gives his to Désirée. The old woman soon moves away, mumbling incomprehensibly. Between her tears and sobs she repeats a litany, from which Michaud can sometimes make out a few words. From time to time tears fall slowly from her eyes, as if she were tired of crying but couldn't help herself. Michaud signals me to stop when I start to move in her direction.

Michaud tries to translate what Désirée says, but his knowledge of Bambara is limited. As a former overseer, he manages to identify the languages of most of the slaves, classifying them rapidly: Mandingo, Wolof, Nago, Mina, Hausa, Ibo, Arada.

"I was head overseer for ten years," he told me one day, "and I can assure you that each of these nations carries its scars not only on their bodies and faces but in its people's gait, in the cadence of their words, in their ways of resisting slavery. But I've never placed labels on the nations like the whites do, calling them sly, brawler, cannibal, or chicken thief. I hit everyone just as hard, never looking at the bent backs, never paying attention to the moans, never showing that I was afraid of their hateful, angry glances, never hesitating or being moved to pity them for the torture the master demanded. This work had to be done, and I did it."

The silence between us alternatively soothes and reopens our wounds. Michaud never speaks of the two attempts to poison him, of the suicide of the Ibo woman who lived with him, of his accident, which happened under more than suspicious circumstances. He is the only one who knows of my relationship with Vincent, a Maroon known as the Fearless One. He knows I know about his role as a messenger, that he is an intermediary for slaves who want to run away, find shelter, and not get captured. But today the news of Paladin's horrific death must have finally made it to the shack, reaching those slaves who no longer can work, for Michaud's voice pours out like cloudy brandy. I don't like the tremors that fill his eyes with pain and the stammering that pulses beneath his skin. I put my hand on his right arm, the one that still fills his sleeve and knocks against his thighs in despairing spasms.

"It must be the weather," I tell him, pointing at the overcast sky. "You know how rain makes your bones tingle."

Michaud doesn't respond right away. I hand him two copies of *L'Affiche Américaine* that I was able to steal without the master's knowledge, but Michaud looks uninterested.

"It's true we can read, you and I," he says with a tone so bitter that, despite myself, I open my mouth to protest, but he doesn't let me speak.

"You think that having taken the risk of teaching other slaves to read makes us any less privileged?"

Michaud's words drench my remorse, which is always ready to overcome any impulse toward fervor by negating it with despair. I choke back all my distress, the unshed tears that flowed within me during the days of cotton and chiffon, at nap time in Mademoiselle Sarah's room while the sun beat high and heavy on the backs of those in the fields, during the warm nights spent at the foot of Mademoiselle Sarah's bed while the cool air made others shiver, despite the sealed windows of the wooden shacks.

"I silence the wounds inflicted by a thousand slaps given with such natural ease, received a thousand times with such apparent submission, that one wonders if they will always be a part of life. I won't mention the weight of the forced smiles, drawing out our dignity until it stiffens. No, I say nothing about this because the scale that can counterbalance shame does not exist.

"It's funny," Michaud continues, his eyes suddenly veiled, "but I can't remember what my life was like when I had two arms. It seems that I only began to act when this one was gone, when I felt the weight of a falling arm, chopped off, still alive, bleeding and jolting. I know the slaves talk about it on the plantation. Me, I never said anything. Today Lisette, let me tell you the story of the arm I no longer have."

I hardly dared to breathe as I waited for Michaud to continue, my eyes fixed on his fairly calm face.

"That was the day," he said, "they brought back Arcinte, a Nago woman who had already tried to escape once; the coachman had caught her and taken her back to the master Fayot. He isn't meaner than anyone else, but maybe he had slept badly or dreamed of Negroes' blood the night before. I know that at the time he was chasing Josette, a freedwoman, a seamstress on Rue 10, who only had eyes for her man, Ti Jean. You know how the master goes crazy over a well-rounded, small woman."

Gracieuse's small, round silhouette closing the door to the master's large room weaves into my memory, and I nod my head to tell Michaud I know what he's talking about. This penchant of the master's had kept me out of his indiscreet hands. Too bad his son didn't share his father's tastes
. . .

My mind turns this page quickly, and I let Michaud's words continue their long pilgrimage.

"I think," he said, "she would have preferred that they branded her again and cut off an ear, like they did the first time. But the master ordered fifty lashes of the *rigoise** for Arcinte, twenty-nine as stipulated in their *Code noir* and twenty-one more to dissuade her from giving in to the desire to run away a third time. She was seven months pregnant, and I knew that she'd had two miscarriages already. She was about thirty years old, calm and determined, never a complaint from her. She carried her dreams in her eyes. A dream made up of two branches closely intertwined: to have a child and to be free. Her last attempt at escaping had cost her not only an ear but her child as well. She had the marks of the mastiffs' bites on her calves. Her baby's father had escaped, and obviously she wanted to join him. But I think her need for freedom was not linked to any man; in slavery she simply could not breathe. The master ignored my suggestion that he give her a different punishment. They had undressed the woman already, dug a hole big enough to accommodate her naked belly. When they had placed her against the ground, her naked buttocks exposed, Arcinte let out a cry that begged for madness to destroy her."

Once again, Michaud stops, and I see his lips tense. Powerless, I can only wait for him to find the strength to continue.

"You see, Lisette, if she had gone completely mad, I would have said that she had not understood, that in her confusion she had seen herself as a bird of paradise with her son on her wings and a flower in her beak. But her cry cast over me a chill reminiscent of early-morning mist. I knew that every fiber of her being was weeping for her lost child.

---

* A whip made of woven straps of leather invented to discipline slaves working on plantations.

Her child was already a slave and punished before birth, forever marked by the whip of the overseer—my whip!—I, the one who daily beat, whipped, and punished. Don't ask me how I could do it because to this day I wonder if it wasn't my guardian angel who dealt the blow. Don't tell anyone that I think I used the machete that I always kept by my side because I will deny it. My left wrist fell neatly and evenly. I felt the pain lodged at the tip of my five remaining fingers. I don't know what the master or the others did with all the blood and that member that no longer belongs to me.

"I muster my strength and turn to look at Arcinte, who gets up and goes. She is no longer naked, someone must have given her a shirt, beneath which her buttocks protrude, devoid of any sexuality. She leaves, shaking as she silently sobs, leaning on two other women who carry her more than lead her away. Then, relieved, I close my eyes, and beneath my pupils used to seeing hidden smiles, I see Arcinte, a free, elongated silhouette moving toward the hills, her son in her arms, without chains or bites, infinitely female in the beauty of her sex. The pain in me dances a frenetic and merciless *congo*, and I let myself go."

Michaud pauses for a brief moment, and I see from his serene gaze that he has gone to the free spaces occupied by Arcinte. He smiles before continuing. "To explain this accident, people spoke of vengeful gods, of vodun, of punishment deserved. After that the master cast me on this dump with all the others deemed useless . . . It's been three years now."

Between us silence covers the wounds with a veil of peace and a soft breeze. Michaud's right hand seems very heavy to me today. Grandma Charlotte's memory weighs on me. I remember her words from long ago telling me about her capture, the time in the barracoons, when she was sold and burned. After each of our encounters filled with love and pain, she would tell me: "Your story must dwell, vigilant, under your skin, at the tips of your hair. Each piece that you add to it grows roots and stars for your dreams."

Michaud's tale glides over me and joins all the other pieces of stories around and inside me, leaving me both satisfied and infinitely sad.

AS I LEAVE MICHAUD, I FEEL the need to touch my talisman, to see these things that link me to Grandma Charlotte, to my mother, whom I didn't know, and to this great-aunt Brigitte they spoke so much about to me. I suffer from all the mysteries that surround me, from the stories that reveal themselves as pain comes and goes, from the days ahead that seem to extend immense tentacles of despair and anger. Despite Vincent's confident words and Michaud's usual serenity, which returned after he told the story of his amputated arm, the reign of terror saturates the atmosphere and fills me with gloom.

Each day at the master's table, I sense their fear in the way they nervously pour their drinks, peering at the contents as they hold up the glasses even after they're finished; the way they grip the glasses a little too tightly and set them down loudly, abruptly, on the tablecloth. At the last dinner the master hosted, his neighbor Monsieur Villiers was as usual the most agitated and violent one in the group.

"We must take drastic, punitive measures, and above all, we mustn't let them see our fear."

"But we are afraid," Déracine's wife protested—her husband was currently away on a trip to France. "Bernard has just left. He promised he'd return as soon as possible, but it will be at least four months."

No one mentioned outwardly the war raging between France and England and the risks the French ships were taking, but I knew everyone was thinking about it. Déracine had thought for a long time before taking this trip.

"We must have an iron fist," insisted Villiers, who was least inclined to focus on other people's problems. "There'll be no expression of compassion, like the Pelletier imbecile, who wouldn't burn his coachman."

"Come on, he had worked for him for twelve years!" my mistress exclaimed.

"So what? Don't you know that most of the poisoners are among the slaves who are closest to us?"

"Are they really to blame?" asked Madame Déracine, her voice filled with doubt. "We're so afraid, we're not thinking clearly anymore."

Guilty or not, in the space of three weeks they've burned a coachman, two cooks, and a servant. Each week brings news of other poisonings from almost every part of the region. Animals die. Men take to their beds only to die a day or a few hours later. My memory is already full of so many dead! A persistent anguish steals into my heart as I confront this new menace along with the torture and beatings from which one does not recover, the suicides, the escapes, and the fatal illnesses, one after the other, starting in the dry season and continuing all the way into the rainy season.

I'm afraid for Vincent, my love from the endless hills; for Michaud, with his dignity no machete can crush. I'd like to be sure that nothing will separate me from Ma Augustine, who all by herself stands for Grandma Charlotte, my great-aunt Brigitte, and all my ancestors who died in the prime of their lives. Sometimes, when I look at Ma Victor, I wonder if she has forgotten that the cooks were the first to be punished at the slightest suspicion of poisoning. Little Manon plays roulette with death every day—one spoonful for Madame, one for Monsieur, and if it's not swell, I go straight to hell. I'm ashamed when her eyes meet mine. All these children around me whose lives mean so little: little Mariette, daughter of Louise the washerwoman, who works with Mam'zelle Jeanne; Joséphine, the little mulatto who is Clarisse's daughter.

I'm worried about Fontilus, my friend from our days of running around butt-naked. When we were children, we used to hide sometimes in the tree where I stashed my valuables. Fontilus, my funny friend with the sad eyes, who told me yesterday morning: "Dad thinks I'm twenty-five now. Isn't it crazy to keep track of your age when you're a slave? Shouldn't we all swallow our tongues like the Ibo woman who killed herself last month? Why don't you kiss me, and we'll die together, my dear Lisette?"

I admit to worrying even about Gracieuse the cocotte, whose ambiguous smile sends me into a rage at times.

Nestled among the leaves of the tree, I take the talismans out from their hiding place. As if telling beads, I roll the roughly tied knots on Aunt Brigitte's cord between my fingers. I've washed this cord, made of scraps of worn, unbleached linen, over and over without understanding why Grandma Charlotte and my godmother looked at it with that fascinating mix of veneration and repulsion they tried in vain to hide from me.

"You're still too young to understand," my grandmother told me again when I asked her about it with my words, a look, or a gesture. And she would tell me other stories to fill my eyes, to satisfy my hands, seeking answers with my two clenched fists. She knew that I'd stay there for hours, daydreaming, if she talked to me about those long-ago times, about my mother and aunt Brigitte.

All her remarks began the same way: "Ayouba, your mother, had not yet understood the meaning of her destiny when the horror began. We were about twenty people, young men, beautiful and strong, young women, full of life, with high and beautiful chests, laughing eyes, and promising hands. Free. Brigitte could have told you how we were captured, how we resisted. Me, I only want to remember the simple joy that existed before, before the smell of those waves, those winds, and the sand moving beneath our feet. I don't just want to remember sand dunes and the bare shoulders of slaves. I want to think about the time before the kidnapping, before *The Infamous Rosalie*. Because afterward I'll have nothing warm to hold in my memory, except the weight of your hand against my cheek the day of your birth."

After starting to tell the story, Grandma Charlotte always respected a moment of silence. I appreciated this pause, which brought us together and gave me permission to choose my story for that day. Grandmother would agree to my request, except when I demanded she tell Brigitte's story or the one about the barracoons that she was keeping for a special day, a day still to come . . .

"Tell the story about *The Infamous Rosalie*, Grandma Charlotte."

"First, there was this camp, which was like an enormous ditch surrounded by fencing. One day, I promise you, I'll tell you about the barracoons; one day, when you'll need wings to carry yourself beyond the present moment. One day, when your need will be greater than my fear of going back there in my memory. But not today . . .

On the ship I experienced a night I had never known, a night with no sky, no stars, no breeze; with bodies huddled against each other; without love or passion; with odors and movements stripped of their intimacy; with linked embraces and never-ending moans. Imagine a night when you can't count the stars because above you is nothing but a wooden ceiling. In place of windows were panels. In place of a universe was steerage. At night our bodies and minds do not rest, and shadows heighten the sense of turmoil caused by flesh pressing into flesh. You spend several days with your breath in tune to that of your companion in chains when you realize her breathing has ceased and that you're bound to a nearly rigid corpse. And no one hears your scream; it resonates only in your ears and heart . . .

For there are hundreds of screams that mask your own. When you finally see the light of day, the smell of the vinegar used to wash the deck turns the ocean surrounding you into an enormous burning field that blinds and chokes you. Not even the sun had ever seemed as cruel or merciless. When the weather's nice and they decide we've endured the frigid, moldy ship's hold long enough, when the dampness of our intermingled breaths has grown hot enough, just when our fear has plumbed the depths of terror, they take us out on the deck. Then it's time to wash up. They gather us together and throw water on us. Sometimes, in spite of yourself, you let yourself be taken by the softness of the water on your skin. This familiar contact makes you forget everything for one sweet second that, with your eyes closed, you wish lasted forever. Then, just when you've begun to believe that you still have a heart lodged deep in a body that is no longer yours, they command you to run and dance. So to the tune of their cruelty and our distress, our feet rise and fly about. With each movement our tears and our sweat become one."

I knew what was coming, but by that point I couldn't keep my eyes from growing wet as Grandma Charlotte continued her story.

"One day when they gave us glasses full of brandy, a young Hausa woman, whose name I never learned, danced Don Pedro's dance. The whites laughed, but we all knew she was conjuring death. She and her man danced face to face, both of them so young and beautiful. Two 'pretty bolts of India cloth,' as the men and women between the ages of eighteen and twenty-five who had all their teeth were called. Brigitte and I were like so many of the others who had been captured with us, bolts of India cloth that could sell for up to two thousand pounds apiece. Especially Brigitte, so tall, so beautiful, so proud—my older sister, whose very skin changed the day they caught her on the coast! May the Good Lord forgive her! . . .

"So that afternoon this young Hausa woman began to dance with her man. She was bidding farewell to the land she had left behind and that she'd never see again; to the stars and the moon, whose light never reached the depths of the ship's hold; to love, which had lost its appetite for light; to the children she would not bear; to the sky and sea that promised her freedom. Her steps were pounding our senses, and we beat our hands and feet, embracing her with courage and dignity. The music was becoming more and more violent, and the two bodies crashed into each other, grazing then turning away from each other with similar movements, filled with pain and rage. The whites were laughing. Afraid yet fascinated, they were inventing thousands of fantasies. Then the drumming of our hands and feet stopped cold. In the same spirit the man and the woman sprung forward and threw themselves into the sea. Mixed with the sailors' cries and confused gestures were the groans and snarls that tangled up our words and the fury of the captain, who watched as the sea and its sharks caught the two bodies, so reducing his profit. He sent us back to the ship's steerage, men between the rear mast and the forecastle, women and children under the sternpost.

"After that they chained those of us they deemed dangerous. Brigitte was the first to be chosen. I always thought Brigitte would have found a way to kill herself; the fact that she didn't do it by taking a good number of them with her was no doubt because of your mother and me . . .

"There were those among us who let ourselves die without a sound. They sat down, placed their chins on their knees, then closed their eyes and stopped up their ears. It was as if they were refusing to let life enter through any orifice. They rejected food and drink and patiently waited for death.

"I tell you, Lisette, when you've lived through the barracoons and the crossing, the sale and every possible hue of shame, even when you continue to breathe, large pieces of you are lost forever, like strips of flesh you've scraped off, one after another. In the end you're so torn apart you no longer feel a thing. You're imprisoned in a shell no ray can penetrate. You know, Augustine was there with us. She was still a little girl, all skinny, without much commercial value. Three slave children were worth one bolt of India cloth— but she was part of our group, Brigitte's and mine. Your mother too. We all came on the same ship. Our men stayed back there in our country, Brigitte's as well as mine. For a long time I wondered what they would have done if they'd been with us that morning. No doubt, they would've been killed too, just like Brigitte's two sons, who were killed in front of us because they were defending themselves and trying to protect us. They were beautiful, sturdy boys with strong legs and fearless, flawless hands. Their bodies stayed behind on the coast. My poor sister fought like a shrew to stay with them. They hit her so hard and for so long she lost consciousness, which is how they carried her onto the ship, *The Infamous Rosalie*.

I had noticed Grandma Charlotte's branding several times before, as I had Ma Augustine's: TR on their right breast. *The Rosalie*. The place where the unspeakable had occurred. I see the branding now, as Ma Augustine drops her tired, old bones on our makeshift mattresses, old straw mats made of corn. Since Grandma Charlotte's death and Mademoiselle Sarah's departure, I sleep with Ma Augustine. The night is ours, just ours alone. It's when we stretch our toes, stretch our arms against our hips, and look inward without pretending otherwise. I hold Ma Augustine's hands in mine, and they remind me that my godmother must be in her fifties. Her skin has experienced years of slavery, the big house, and all the work that gnaws away at our bones and our lives. Her long fingers, bent by frequent pain, resemble old tools beyond repair. I extend them out and relax them, and Ma Augustine dozes off. I can tell by her breathing, which echoes the soft breeze brushing past me, reaching me from afar. It's as if in order to sleep better she has to retreat to a milder climate. I look at my godmother's face, which even in rest tells me clearly that life has marked it with a thousand wounds and that her face responded to each blow in kind. Every wrinkle and crack tells the story of a challenge, an injury, a conflict. No prayer, no forgiveness.

After seeing Vincent and hearing Michaud's tale, I need this moment of tenderness with my godmother. Even when she's asleep, just knowing of her affection for me is a reassurance. Suddenly her eyes open, at once suspicious and loving. Ma Augustine always catches me by surprise; I'm never sure that she's fully asleep.

"Be careful, Lisette. People are more attentive than you think."

It's just like Ma Augustine to let me know, in a few words, that she knows of my meetings. I don't know if I ought to respond.

As usual after these moments of rest, Ma Augustine sits down so I can comb her hair. Today we can't sit outside. Gusts of rain are knocking against the shack's fence. Drops fall on us through the roof thatched with leaves. She puts an old, worn sheet over her shoulders, while the smell of the ginger tea I made permeates the room. It's our time of rest and complicity. My fingers trace the paths where we keep our secrets and confessions in her thick, gray locks. I rub her scalp and put castor oil in her hair for a long time with long, soothing, affectionate movements of my hands. I flatten, cajole, and gather her hair, making one neat mound after another for her.

"I'm afraid of Gracieuse, Godmother. I don't know what she wants."

"Child, she wants what we all want," Ma Augustine sighs. "It's not easy being the mistress of a colonist, especially with his Creole wife on the premises. Gracieuse made a pact with her body. I don't know which one will wear out first!"

Ma Augustine lets me ponder her cryptic words. Like Grandma Charlotte always said, life decides when the moment will come and not a minute sooner; pray to the Good Lord that it doesn't come a second too late.

"Talk to me about my father, Godmother."

"But I've already told you everything about him, Lisette."

Ma Augustine knows well that this is my favorite ploy for trying to get more information about that time she and Grandma Charlotte have shrouded in mystery. It begins with their arrival on the island and goes up to their sale to Fayot. This is when my aunt Brigitte died. What does their silence mean—this silence that intrigues and confounds me? I try to make up for it by gathering the small bits of information that I collect here and there from Grandma Charlotte and Ma Augustine over the years.

"When Charlotte, your mother, and I left the Montreuil plantation, your mother was several months pregnant. You were born, as you already know, here on this plantation. Your mother, who was very young and frail, couldn't fight the fatigue caused by the voyage and labor. She died shortly afterward. It was another young Ibo woman who nursed you. Her own baby died before turning one. As soon as you stopped nursing, she disappeared. We heard that she threw herself from the top of the cliff near the woods in Limbé. Your father, a Nago man, had already been killed with other Maroons who had attacked a crew on the road to Limonade. Your grandmother loved your father very much; she would tell me that his voice was as strong as a torrent running down a mountainside. She called him Storm. He loved your mother and would lift her in the air and twirl her around. She would hold on with both hands and laugh her light, fragile laugh. She looked so sad that sometimes it was almost painful to see her happy."

While my hand wanders through Ma Augustine's graying hair, I tell myself that sometimes life gives us lessons we could do without. I was fourteen years old when Grandma Charlotte died, old and weakened, helpless in the face of the smallpox that killed her. Slavery had depleted my grandmother's reserves of joy and tenderness. She had only her anger and pride left. I learned to respect the distance she imposed on everyone who got close to her, but I knew that I was her most prized possession in the world.

"I'm not ready to live without Grandma Charlotte," I had said to Ma Augustine.

"You will have to be," replied the one who had made the voyage with my grandmother from the distant coast of Africa in the steerage of *The Infamous Rosalie*, by way of the barracoons.

Several months later it was Ma Augustine once again who took me in her arms when I returned from the big house with my legs streaked with blood and sticky liquid, with moist eyes and a trembling mouth.

"Was it the master or Monsieur Raoul?" she asked simply.

"Monsieur Raoul," I stammered, trying to chase away the imprint of the white hands inside me. "I bit him on the arm," I added, spitting in disgust.

I felt Ma Augustine's smile on my forehead, and I saw her tears fall for the first time. Then she lifted my face toward her and wiped it with her apron.

"You're an Arada woman, and you will always be: the white man's fingers can never take away the mark of your race. Your race is in the whites of your eyes, and you will die with it, just like your great-aunt Brigitte, your grandmother Charlotte, and your mother."

"And like you, Ma Augustine."

"Yes, like me."

That day my godmother gave me a bath in the middle of the day, behind the shack. With leaves and roots whose smell lingered on my skin, she dabbed my body, my thighs and between my thighs, my buttocks, all of my parts. A month later the young master Raoul caught a terrible itch—and no one knew how—that kept him in bed, wearing no pants, no underwear, emitting plaintive cries that were received with nods of understanding in the kitchen and during church services. That night I kneeled in front of Ma Augustine and lay my grateful head on her knees.

"An eye for an eye, a tooth for a tooth, is that it?"

"It doesn't always work like that. Marks vary," she told me. "Some accompany you and disfigure you, and I'm not talking about the one on my right breast. We have to scrub a long time to rediscover the spring in our step that we had before, so our feet experience once more the magic of the sun and the caress of dawn."

Five years later bile rises in my throat when I think of Raoul's face breathing next to mine, his shirt opened to reveal his reddish torso, his thighs knocking against mine, his fingers searching my sex, paying no mind to my cries, my tears, or my sobbing. I feel the rage and hatred take over my sadness and settle into righteous anger. At the moment my anger is like calm water, a light breeze with no protection. But do we have any other choice than to accept the showers and the torrential rains, the earthquakes, when everything changes place and season?

As soon as I enter the big house the next day, I sense a strange agitation that has nothing to do with Ma Victor's comings and goings from the kitchen to the chapel nor with the tubs and baskets of dirty laundry the washerwoman's beginning to soak in water. First of all, the mistress isn't in bed. I hear her calling my name, this woman who doesn't wake up until well after the plantation master leaves. This woman who takes her breakfast in bed: coffee, a few pieces of fruit, and bread with jam. I see the rose and perfumed lace of her bed jacket flapping against the nearby furniture.

"Hurry up, Lisette. Go help Gracieuse get everything ready—we're going to town."

Just like that, all of a sudden? Normally, the mistress has her dress and ornaments laid out the night before. My look of surprise contrasts with Gracieuse's utterly relaxed manner. Her steps, scarcely less lethargic than usual, lead from the wardrobe to the suitcases, from the bed to the dressing table. The drawers are opened, the trunks closed, jewelry is chosen with a "yes, mistress" and murmurs of approval. I am suddenly overcome with the desire to shake Gracieuse

33

and strike her rounded shoulders rolling under the scarf around her neck. The mistress's careless words make me finally understand that because of the problems on some plantations in the area, the planters have decided to leave the colony, for a while or altogether. The mistress had decided to go into town to get news and visit some neighbors. Little Mariette arrives to say that the coachman is ready to drive Madame. I barely listen to the orders the mistress is issuing from across the room.

"Prepare my new outfit, the blue one. No, Gracieuse, I told you several times I don't wear those shoes to go into town! Take this pair of court shoes instead. Lisette, come arrange my earrings. Mariette, take the parasol that matches the dress. Go get dressed, Gracieuse and Lisette, you know very well that you're accompanying me. Mariette, warn Joséphine, you know how slow that girl is! Tell Jeannine she's coming with us. And tell her not to put too much makeup on today!"

The mistress likes to surround herself with beautiful people when she goes into town. Her cocotte Gracieuse is all elegant, her fine traits befitting a brown wax doll. I, Lisette: Charlotte's granddaughter, a "pure specimen of the Gold Coast," as the neighbor Villiers says, "high-chested with the legs of a gazelle and the buttocks of a pregnant woman"; Mariette, with her long black hair and her toasted almond–colored eyes; and Joséphine, daughter of the quadroon Clarisse, who's responsible for all the fine pastries for parties and balls, make up Madame's typical entourage, for each outing is an opportunity to be seen. This morning the mistress saw fit to have Jeannine, a Creole woman with golden skin, whose lively and heavy breasts never fail to attract men's gaze, accompany us. Fayot brought her back from a trip to Petit-Gôave. Fontilus told me the coachman told him that the master won Jeannine in a poker game with a planter from Petit-Gôave whose vice-ridden blood is weak for women like Jeannine. In any case, as soon as she laid her eyes on the young woman, the mistress brought her into her service under Gracieuse's supervision. The cocotte, no doubt confident of her power over Fayot, showed no jealousy and welcomed Jeannine with the same nonchalance she brings to every endeavor. Actually, I think Gracieuse was right not to get upset. Even if sometimes the master caresses Jeannine's breasts in passing, he seems to do it more to show his proprietary right than for pleasure.

Gracieuse came back with one of the mistress's old skirts she must have been given long ago, since I'd never seen her wear it. She put on a fine batiste blouse and a pretty bonnet but didn't dare keep the double row of lace that adorned it. Jeannine put on another blouse whose opening revealed her budding breasts beneath the fine cotton shift she threw over her shoulders.

"Hurry up," she told me, her voice betraying a singsongy accent.

I ran to our shack to change clothes. I vigorously scrubbed my face and neck and behind my ears with an old piece of soap from the mistress that I keep for these occasions. The smell of jasmine endures in the dry, cracked shell of soap. When I return to the big house, I meet Ma Augustine, who immediately stares at the gold pendant earrings I'm wearing.

"You know very well," Ma Augustine had told me, all surprised, when I showed her the pendant earrings Mademoiselle Sarah had given me the eve of her departure, "we don't have the right to wear gold jewelry. You have your *rassade* necklace and your silver bracelet. That should be more than enough."

"Fayot doesn't want us going to church after Mass either," I mutter.

I know Ma Augustine and other slaves—the women especially—get together with Father Clément rather frequently. He's an old, bent Jesuit priest who, from the planters' perspective, is wrong to treat slaves like they are human beings. Returning home from these meetings, my godmother walks with a heavy step, as if the ideas exchanged had burdened her back, but her face shines with the memory of a thousand forbidden, liberating, and disturbing thoughts. Similarly, my eyes often reach for the mountains' colors, which are immune to these bans that cut life short. How do I explain that blue and white, the colors reserved for slaves, sap my strength? I dream of dancing, covered in lace and flounce, in an endless orgy of colors, of clinking golden necklaces, of puffy sleeves and blooming blouses. These poor little earrings Mademoiselle Sarah gave me as a last gesture of generosity, marked with the fear of leaving her well-ordered life, are mere bits of sparks I cling to. Forbidden or not, I'm wearing them anyway. Besides, the mistress does not object: what is most important to her is that her slaves, her cocottes, make her proud. She would even go so far as to pay a fine should the constabulary insist on it. She won't prevent me from wearing the earrings. Should I explain all of this to Ma Augustine once again? I let my disavowed desires soak in her quiet wisdom full of hidden stirrings.

"You know, Godmother, that it's more than that . . ."

"I know, Lisette. Church is more than that too."

On the main street we are immersed in noise and movement. Gracieuse's face loses its usual indifference. Subtly, with her eyes, she watches the most beautiful women, assessing their choice of clothes and shoes. She is fascinated by the mulattresses and takes note of their slightest gestures. Jeannine doesn't try to hide her joy, letting it shine in the generous smile that lights up her face. From the seat of her red velvet chair, the mistress points the way, which I communicate to the coachman. It's all about drawing attention to the group's opulence. Everyone knows that Fayot's sugarcane plantations are the most prosperous, that the master has sent his two children to study in Nantes, from which he gets cases of pickle and jam, and that he regularly receives barrels of wine from Bordeaux, not counting Madame's shoes and hats. Mariette is the first to get out and holds the coach door open, and I follow with the parasol. Gracieuse helps the mistress set one foot on the ground, then the other one. Joséphine, with her long brown hair, and Jeannine, with her copper skin, bring up the rear of our procession. We begin to parade through the market's passageways, Gracieuse on the left, I on the right, Jeannine and the young ones behind.

This is how we stroll through the stalls, past the sellers of trinkets and the small merchants, stopping as the mistress' whim and curiosity dictate. We walk along, strolling with the same nonchalance, for we must never appear like we're rushed nor give the impression that we are worried in the least. Pricking up my ears, I nevertheless hear bits of conversation that burst from all sides as I move with headstrong confidence and a lively stride. If the mistress decides that one of us is dishonoring her procession, she bans her from the next outing. So I hold my chin up and make the petticoat of my skirt flow with each step.

"The constabulary imprisoned ten rebellious Negroes."

"They'll be executed in the town square."

"*The African* finally arrived, the day before yesterday, because they had mechanical problems in the crossing. To prevent starvation, the captain had to throw twenty-seven Negroes overboard."

"We burned the Negro Brutus alive—he's from the Lalanne plantation. Another one of those poisoners! It seems that he poisoned five Negroes and his overseer, a mulatto."

The news spreads among the town dwellers as they come and go: small-time, swindling white planters and freed slaves trying to sell their wares.

"Mesdemoiselles, silk scarves and soap from Paris. Rice powder for your cheeks, Mesdames."

Workers offer their services: a joiner skilled in fabrication and repair; a wigmaker who can comb your hair in the latest style from Paris.

I store all important information, filing it immediately into categories of good and bad, keeping them in the back of my mind to share later with Ma Augustine, Michaud, and Vincent.

"Flore went back, but the second lieutenant has set up house with a mulatta from Plaisance. People are even saying he intends to marry her."

"The free Negro Richemond was sentenced to fifty lashes in the town square and a hundred days in prison. He was hiding runaway slaves in his house."

"The Congo Marie was captured in L'Acul. She ran away from her master's house twelve years ago."

They caught a runaway Negro who could speak French near Limbé."

I had just filed away this piece of information away when it resonates in me and reverberates down to my lower belly, where it lands with a dull thud. No, Good Lord, not Vincent! What did you do? How could you let this misfortune strike me? Vincent! I can no longer feign my appointed-Negress-from-the-Fayot-plantation face, former servant to Mademoiselle Sarah. I drop my mask of the attractive Creole woman—even in the fluttering of my eyelids, whose tendency to look toward freedom I learned to control at an early age. I abandon my lace-and-crinoline smile, my gait of intoxicating fruit, and my light legs. I'm ready to stamp out my terror.

A sharp pain on the tips of my toes brings me back to earth.

"Look where you're going, my sweetie," Gracieuse tells me.

She's planted her parasol on my bare toes and her melodious voice has never sounded sweeter.

"They caught Milord, the Maroon Milord they've been looking for all this time."

Milord. She said Milord. My breath comes to me in small grateful spurts, and I take it in warily, as if my caution could help dispel bad omens.

That night I still can't shake the gruesome weight of those images of burned bodies swollen with water, floating on frothy waves. Ma Victor so often says Arada women have the power to foresee misfortune. Could it be true? Why do I feel this strange uneasiness, like the threat of rain with no forewarning wind, an unlocatable itch, or a shooting pain playing hide-and-seek in my body? Only Vincent's warm embrace could possibly make me forget the cold shack and its unpleasant stench. Next to me I hear Ma Augustine's breathing, now somewhat more pronounced. Did she get pneumonia, like Ti Marie did a year ago? A deafening anguish moves me to touch her hand lightly. Warm and rough, it reassures me for a second before other equally terrifying possibilities rush to assault me.

When I was young, stories of monsters haunted my nights and left me drenched in sweat. I would wet my straw mattress, and often in the early hours of dawn Grandma Charlotte would wash and dry our tattered sheets. In the foggy darkness of the shack, my imagination fueled by the sound of tree branches hitting the boards, I would see terrible beings, cruel and menacing things. How these monsters from childhood seem innocuous to me now, compared to today's anguish! So much distress to ward off, so many lives in which hope and anger tangle together. Am I the only one who perceives suffering and bitterness in Fontilus's laughter? It has been several months now since my companion from the calendas and festive Sundays changed. Of course his feet still defy drum and space. I'm still the only one who can follow his surges and whirls, his jumps and bows. Even as a little girl, taken with the fascinating complicity Fontilus had with music, I begged him to teach me to dance like him. Over time my body learned to move in sync with his. When Fontilus and I dance, we know the exact moment when one loses oneself in the body's exhilaration. It's been a while now since the dances no longer draw my friend into that enchanted world of maddening and rebellious rhythms. The sadness in his eyes doesn't dampen his steps, but it leaves me full of worry. I know Fontilus's dreams, I feel them in his arms as they twirl and catch me effortlessly; I know the speed of his legs, which never stumble, not even in the most strenuous dances. So often, with a bright, faraway look in his eyes, he would talk to me about a future we had to create.

Fontilus apprenticed for three months with Talbot, the mason, a spotty and sickly white man, who turned red all over when he coughed. I overhead Fayot whisper to the mistress that Talbot should thank the colony for having made him so rich, as he barely knew how to read. Indeed, Talbot is now the owner of a plantation with slaves under his watch. Fontilus learned his trade with him, and now it's been five years since the master lets him do small jobs for other planters who have no masons on their property. Fayot, always eager, naturally, to make a profit, demanded that Fontilus give him forty piastres a month. At first Fontilus didn't complain. I watched him supervise dozens of field slaves repairing the Negroes' shacks. He built a stable for sick horses for Villiers and a storehouse for the Delermes. The master says that having a mason slave on his plantation increases its value, and that's why he agreed to let Fontilus learn the trade with Talbot this entire time.

The glow in Fontilus's eyes has died out since he started meeting with Léandre, the mulatto who belongs to Lambert, the tapestry maker.

"You know Léandre's been working as a master carpenter for nine years now. He hopes to buy his freedom, but every month he has nothing left after he pays his master. Each month Léandre invents new chains that will forever keep him a slave. He has to repair the Negroes' shacks and redo the roof of the *guildiverie*.* He has to expand the carriage house, but he'll never be able to collect the sum he needs to buy his freedom. And he's a mulatto after all! So, can you imagine how difficult it would be for me, a Congo *bossale* man?! Even though I arrived here seven years ago, I am and will always be a *bossale*. I'll never be able to buy my freedom."

I tried to comfort Fontilus, in vain.

"As Ma Victor says, you're strong, Fontilus. There aren't many young *bossale* Negroes who survive here in Saint-Domingue. You've made it through illness, the climate, mosquitoes, and whippings. You grew up here, learned a trade. Don't let yourself get discouraged! Don't forget that Léandre works for a small-time white planter. You know they have the reputation of being the toughest."

Fontilus didn't even bother to argue with me. With a resigned sigh, he said, "Lisou, when a house falls down, you don't accuse the window of not closing properly!"

My companion from the calendas and festive days left for a world where I can no longer join him. His laughter reached me covered in ash.

Once I spoke about Fontilus's dreams to Michaud. The former overseer with the vengeful arm waited a long time before speaking, then he said: "Never explain to a man being whipped how to avoid blows. Every one learns to protect

* A distillery where spirits are made from sugarcane.

42

the body part most sensitive to him, his most vital part. You'll see all sorts of ruses that we slaves invent to try to survive this horror. Some will seem ridiculous, others barbaric, but who can really judge? A human being will do whatever he needs to do to make sure the breath that fills his voice belongs to him. It's his right."

IT IS BECOMING HARDER AND HARDER to predict whom the mistress will slap, to whom she will offer a gesture of generosity, or on whom she will shine her incandescent smile. Little Joséphine is slapped, shoved, and whipped with the hairbrush and whip. Even in moments of serenity, as she lays in the hammock under the almond tree, the mistress is still hostile to Joséphine. It seems that Clarisse had this tender, green-eyed little girl with Malary, who had sold both of them to the Fayots before leaving the colony. I remember when the master bought this lot of slaves three years ago already. He knew the servants, having visited the Malary plantation frequently: Clarisse and Joséphine, Ma Thérèse, the coachman Gabriel, and Ti Marie, a washerwoman who died of pneumonia shortly thereafter. But for the fifteen or twenty field slaves, it was a whole other story. The master doesn't mix business with pleasure.

I had accompanied them to the Malary plantation. Gracieuse and I were watching the scene as we held a parasol and fan for the mistress, who insisted on being present during the transaction. The master carefully examined the slaves he deemed to be risky. Belin, the manager, was also there. They asked the Negroes to open their mouths and inspected their nearly naked bodies. The master went so far as to feel the women's buttocks while he exchanged pleasantries with Malary. There were eight women in this lot of field slaves. One of them had brands and scar burns all over her body. Her breasts hung long and slack, and her hair had fled her temples to gather in a tousled tuft on the top of her head. I looked away from this woman, but despite myself, my eyes returned to linger on her scarred face. Belin, the thrifty one, felt her all over, then asked her to jump as he watched her stomach tossing up and down. He shook his head. The woman turned her imploring yet already resigned eyes toward Fayot, who, with a single gesture of his hand, brushed this unpleasant image from his mind and indicated that he did not want her.

I don't know what became of this woman. She was undoubtedly sold with the other rejects to Chatelin, who was known for his savagery. His name alone is enough to spread panic among slaves. Many masters prevail over recalcitrant ones by threatening to sell them to Chatelin. He's the one who recently tortured a Negress accused of having aborted voluntarily. He burned her thighs and legs until she confessed the name of the midwife who had helped her. Chatelin then had them both burned slowly. They died a long, horrible death. Apparently, there was an investigation, but Chatelin's neighbors and the members of the council didn't want to impose sanctions on one of their own. This was the way they prevented slaves from becoming too rebellious. Villiers spoke about it among the masters: "Chatelin may have gone overboard. We all know he's rather brutal and boorish, but the council's decision not to sanction him is wise. Each man must be able to take the law into his own hands! Otherwise, we won't be able to put a stop to the Negroes' revolts."

And so the colonists who find themselves obliged to take leave quickly and sell their slaves run to Chatelin because he rarely refuses to purchase a slave. He knows he'll get his money's worth. Whether ill, old, or handicapped, Chatelin does what it takes to make the slave work. "A Negro must only stop working at his death," he says. What had he done with this woman with the blank stare, who simply lowered her head as we left the Malary plantation?

I remember the mistress sulking on the trip back and long after we reached the plantation.

"I don't know why Joseph bought Clarisse, a stuck-up girl with the airs of a grown woman, and her dull daughter. What a stupid idea to burden oneself with a five-year-old girl who, on top of it all, seems to be retarded!"

The mistress wouldn't stop complaining, and the master remained quiet, as usual. Master Fayot doesn't lose his cool easily. Fontilus whispered to me that the mistress was in love with Malary and she was just jealous of Clarisse. Malary had apparently sworn to Clarisse that she would be freed at his death but because of his many debts, Malary had not been able to keep his promise when he left the colony with his family. It even seemed that Malary owed a considerable amount of money to the master. And so Clarisse had to make do with being sold to Fayot, who had a reputation for being mean but fair to his slaves. She would have her freedom in ten years, according to the conditions agreed upon by the two colonists. When I run into Clarisse in the big house, she often reminds me of a sizzling hot rod. Sometimes Clarisse lowers her long brown eyelashes, and the laughter that bubbles from her perennially painted lips communicates no joy—could it be to hide her bright scarlet anger? Little Joséphine is eight years old now; she will have to wait another seven years before she can escape from the mistress's frustrations. At times, when the slaps and blows fall a little too often, the master pleads in her favor, which sets off a tirade from the mistress.

"I know very well that you too have taken a liking to this quadroon. She's cajoled you, after casting a spell on Adrien Malary. Whenever I touch this bastard of Malary's, you reproach me."

And yet I could have told the mistress a thing or two about her husband's tastes. Me, I don't attract him, my buttocks and waist being too big for him. It's been a while since Jeannine's breasts no longer seem to interest him, except for the occasional petting sessions he partakes in without thinking. He considers Clarisse a beautiful, amusing toy, of which he will soon tire. From time to time he lifts her underskirts and rubs himself against her in the corners of rooms and behind closet doors. In these moments Clarisse bursts into her fresh, sparkling laughter. Once I saw them holed up in one corner of the storeroom, between cases of sausage and barrels of wine. Clarisse ruffled the master's hair and slipped a hand under his shirt, then ran away skipping. When he sees Clarisse, Fayot becomes a young man again, happy and carefree. He is never like this with Gracieuse. His gaze follows the cocotte with the mournful greed of a hand extended for charity that is not forthcoming. Gracieuse's eyes then skim over the master's desire without even grazing the stiff body leaning toward her. Indifferent and mysterious, Gracieuse never rebuffs a caress;

when the master's imperious and agitated hand stops her and wraps itself around her waist, she freezes until the fingers themselves stop moving altogether, futile. Yet the mistress, who must be very well aware of the master's interest in her dear cocotte, never attacks Gracieuse. It's poor Joséphine who has become her favorite target, as if the eight-year-old girl alone could stand for all the skirts turned up by the master.

These days all the slaves in the big house look grumpy and morose because of Joséphine's tears and Madame's punishments. A badly washed spoon brings fifteen lashes of the whip; an overturned but unbroken vase yields twenty-five. The master finally intervenes to put an end to this series of whippings, but he can't altogether do away with the slaps and rebukes. The atmosphere grows heavy with unspoken horrors. Poisonings and fires, rumors of revolts and plots, scare the whites. Several of the masters' acquaintances decide to leave the colony. Many colonists, burdened with debt, have gone bankrupt; others say they can't put up with the island's climate. But the majority are simply scared. Following the numerous departures of whites, announcements for slave sales abound in the copies of *L'Affiche Américaine*: *Nago Negress, about twenty-eight years old, good cook. Ibo Negro, around eighteen years old, good subject, speaks French. Young Negress, nursing, with two-month-old infant, good seamstress. A Negress, from the Congo nation, about ten years old, good washerwoman.*

"Poor management!" declares the master, with the full authority of his nine hundred and fifty-seven acres of land and his twenty-two-year tenure in the colony.

"What are they afraid of?" asks Villiers, indignantly. "Take whatever measures are necessary. Kill a few slaves, and the rest will start behaving. I'm not going to abandon my plantation to a gang of Negroes."

"Come now," Déracine protests, "we should keep from succumbing to barbarity."

But Villiers quiets him quickly.

"You over there, be careful not to confirm your reputation as a Negro-spoiler!"

Nevertheless, the Fayots and their neighbors made their residence and workrooms more secure. Slave meetings and calenda-filled nights were frowned upon and eventually banned. Worried silences punctuate the masters' conversations. A single name returns again and again to cause them anguish and haunt their words. Each time I hear it, I must subdue my true gaze, the one that demands freedom and dignity, for it quickly springs forward with open and trembling wings, heading for sound. They say this name with traces of hatred in their voices, sullying the air with their mistrust. They bring their heads together as if to protect themselves, the women tapping nervously on the tablecloth. The mistress lets out a nervous and agitated laugh that she's acquired, a laugh that seeks to forget dangers but that only manages to exhibit them behind a pane of glass. The name returns with increasing frequency and in its trail leaves the smell of vengeance. Ruddy reflections color the crystal and porcelain; the women's jewelry become heavy, iron neck collars, immense chains to hold the condemned and runaway slaves back. Jangling bracelets evoke grim images of iron rings, of executioners and pyres. A shudder runs through my shoulders and bare arms. It is mixed in with my anguish over not having seen Vincent for months; the name they spit out and whisper fills me with euphoria and fear—prickling my fingers as I carry empty dishes and plates. My suitably lowered eyes imagine the group of angry Negroes and listen for the frightening name of Makandal. A Mandingo sorcerer with power and courage. A one-armed man who inspires rebellion, so they say, and plans to eliminate all whites from Saint-Domingue.

As a Creole, I can barely imagine a plantation without whites, without a master and a mistress. I grew up as Mademoiselle Sarah's Negress, always ensconced in the masters' room, with my mistress's perfume on my skin, traces of her powder on my fingers, and the imprint of her hand on my cheek. I carry the weight of her son's hands in my sex and the brunt of the whip on my back and thighs. The idea of a Saint-Domingue without colonists and without masters, the image of a plantation without a mistress, without Mademoiselle Sarah, without Monsieur Raoul, staggers my mind, and when my hand fills the glasses flawlessly, I'm surprised that this spinning only occurs in my head.

That night, as I get ready to leave the big house, I notice Gracieuse closing the door to the masters' room. I've seen her repeat this gesture so many times, at different moments of the day. Often it takes place after naptime when the master, the mistress, and the cocotte are reunited; it's always after some gift or favor. She hasn't yet seen me, and it's one of the rare times when I can observe Gracieuse without her knowledge. Despite my unease at spying on her like this, the temptation is too strong, and I hide by the corner of the window. The darkness reduces me to one more shade among many in a world of shadows, but I can see her face appear clearly in the light of the lamps posted near the door. A mix of desolation, hatred, and anger, her distress reaches all the way to me and takes me in its grip, captures me. Suddenly I wish I weren't seeing her in this state, but I am unable to move without her seeing me. Her hands travel up and down her hips over and over again, while at the same time her bosom leans forward before jerking itself backward in the next instant, as if to welcome pain and close it up within her. Supplication and defiance. The two combined movements, intense and uninterrupted, create an atmosphere of prayer and supplication, evoking all the angst within me. My eyes get used to her body's cadence, and I feel as if I'm inside her, like an involuntary and anguished pendulum. After she leaves, I still remain prostrate, trapped in her helplessness and confusion.

I don't want to speak with Ma Augustine about Gracieuse's strange behavior, so I'm happy to find she's already asleep. The smell of burning dried cow dung has permeated the shack with its stifling haze, intended to chase away mosquitoes. I leave the door slightly ajar but lay a worn rug, mended many times over, on Ma Augustine's curled-up body. When the cool, damp breeze settles in the crook of one's bones, it's hard to shake it off.

I stand there for a moment, observing my godmother, and the persistent worry I've been fighting moistens my eyes. Curled up asleep, she looks so frail, so tired, as if she has arrived at the end of her life after traveling a long road without any marked rest stops whatsoever. She loses herself to sleep and her body to rest, yet her face communicates the defeat that—despite her undeniable pride—will not show upon waking. The ravages of time showing on her face reflect the abuses of men and Ma Augustine's resistance to the claws of shame. How many blows of the whip does it take before one becomes immune to them?

Grandma Charlotte and Ma Augustine have never mentioned in my presence the time they toiled in the sugar refinery workrooms on the Limonade plantation, before being sold to Fayot. No doubt it's so they don't speak of my mother's death. And indeed, why hadn't Aunt Brigitte—a renowned healer—been able to save her? This is one of those taboo topics that caused Charlotte to purse her lips and loudly suck her teeth, a gesture full of warning. Augustine, on the other hand, has no problem stopping my curiosity cold with a severe look of outrage. Apparently, Brigitte's death seems to be surrounded by particularly tragic circumstances, but I have no way of finding out what may have happened on the Limonade plantation. When Fayot bought them, they comprised the whole lot: Charlotte, Augustine, and my already pregnant mother. The master wanted to surround himself with competent domestic slaves, so he agreed to buy all of them together.

"You see," my grandmother told me, "at the time the Fayots had only been married a few years and that the mistress was even more frivolous than she is now. She barely took care of the children, and Sarah was only three years old. Fayot spent all his afternoons in the workrooms, supervising everything."

When I imagine the master younger and smarter than he is now, I hardly dare think about all that Charlotte and Augustine have had to endure. Fayot is not the kind of man to refrain from claiming and taking what he thinks is his. How many times have I heard him boast in front of his friends that he knows how to get himself elected councillor to the High Council of Cap-Français, that he knows how to use his connections to get out of a difficult situation when dealing with traders and "corrupt officials." One of Fayot's ambitions is to become a trader, even a trader of slaves. There's no question that he won't be satisfied with being just a simple planter; he has to play an important role in the colony. This is why he always insisted on having a house, a wife, children, and servants, for the sake of appearances.

My childhood comes back to me: I would follow Mademoiselle Sarah around since she was the one in whose service I was bound. When I was ten, she turned me into a black doll to suit her whims and needs: at once a confidante and a whipping girl. As we grew older, our roles took on more or less importance and nuance. I became her fashion advisor and beautician, cleaning her nails and ears. I would comb her hair, give her massages, and rub her with lotion made by Grandma Charlotte to keep her skin soft and tender. She told me about her love story with Jérémie, Delerme's nephew, who was here from Bordeaux for vacation. Her first love, her first disillusionment. Shortly before her sudden departure, she was no longer trying to hide the intense attraction that drew her to watch Colin, the Negro who supervised the carpentry workroom. When he was brought in to take the measurements for the cupboards in the kitchen of the big house, Mademoiselle Sarah made sure she was present. At first she probably did not realize how deep her desire for Colin was, having filed it away as yet another fleeting passion, like the ones she'd had once for lacy hats, golden flat shoes, and modest caresses her belly demanded from my fingers the summer she turned fifteen. Ever rebellious, she even demanded that I show an interest in Colin, when my heart then was full for Samuel, who would die of tetanus shortly afterward. Colin did not remain ignorant of Mademoiselle Sarah's ploys, whose passion grew each time she watched an arm transporting mahogany boards, glimpsed a shoulder bared as he worked, saw a leg straining from the movements of a stubborn saw. I'm not sure, but I think they arranged to meet in one of those many pits nature made all by itself. Mademoiselle Sarah often returned exuding a pleasure that turned her eyes into a tender dawn, her rhythmic steps reminiscent of a body still seized by a desire it shared with another body. Once, while helping her to get ready for bed, I saw marks on her thighs that had turned purple. She fingered them with such sensuality that when she felt my eyes on her, she blushed violently. Mademoiselle Sarah was obliged to leave a few weeks later. The eve of her departure she returned from one of her walks when I was no longer accompanying her, with foggy eyes and bite marks all over her body. The few times that I ran into Colin after Mademoiselle Sarah's departure, I saw in his gaze the same absence I'd always noticed when he would look at Mademoiselle Sarah, standing over his wood shavings. He was tortured one day, apparently for attempting to organize a slave revolt in the workrooms. I don't know what became of him. Yet another absence to add to the long list of names!

I realize that it's becoming harder and harder to keep track of the absences around here. The farewells seem to arrive before we have a chance to love. In a different guise death strikes us and leaves big empty spaces around us. We accept pain like a familiar fog that from time to time lifts to let in a new mourning. The most recent loss is superimposed on the preceding one, until a newer loss comes to replace it. Grief accumulates, and in the end we don't know for whom we are crying, since our pain comes from so many sources. Yet on the list of the disappeared there are some who leave their shadows behind, only to return from time to time to remind us that they've lived and that we'll no longer see them.

I never forgot Samuel. He was barely thirteen years old when he died. He was the grandson of Ma Thérèse, who at that time helped Grandma Charlotte in the kitchen. He and I had grown up together, without diapers, our bottoms bare for all to see. As soon as we finished weeding the small garden Grandma Charlotte, Ma Augustine, and Ma Thérèse tended together, we would run away to the woods. By the time we were ten, we had less time together because Samuel had officially become Monsieur Raoul's "boy," and I was increasingly becoming Mademoiselle Sarah's slave. When the master went hunting, it was Samuel who chased after the game. Ma Thérèse loved her grandson, whom her daughter Julie had left her when she died in childbirth. She was so afraid Samuel would get hit by a stray bullet that she had the solitary habit of muttering prayers under her breath to the gods of her country. She said them in the Mina language as she tended to the fowl, whose necks would be twisted in preparation for the evening meal. While I was being initiated into the world of underskirts and underwear, delicately juggling Mademoiselle Sarah's whims, I was also missing Samuel and his lopsided smile. In our moments of freedom, when the summer heat chased us from the plantation, Samuel and I would walk through the swamps and run in the rain, defying the *avalasses** and thunder. We would swipe each other on the head and share ripe mangoes. Our wet, naked hands would explore each other's bodies, delighting us with their similarities and differences. We sang about our childhood and the tenderness of our awkward, sweet tongues. Samuel was injured while hunting with the master. It seemed to be just a superficial wound, which Ma Thérèse healed with the help of the surgeon Dessalles, but my playmate lost the gaiety in his laugh. His jaw would stiffen, letting out a crunching sound that twisted his face, making him unrecognizable. Samuel died a few days after that accident.

Since that day, Ma Thérèse stopped her wailing and no longer said a word. Sometimes, even now, all these years later, she emits a shriek that makes men and animals shudder. After Samuel's death, Grandma Charlotte managed to convince the masters that Ma Thérèse could still help her in the kitchen. Then, when it was her turn, Ma Augustine took Ma Thérèse under her wings.

"As long as I don't have to cross her path," the mistress had said. "This woman looks too much like trouble."

It's always hard when my eyes meet Ma Thérèse's, as if I were treading lightly on her pain with my still-awkward ways. I don't know how to turn my desire for happiness into an act of contrition.

The day Samuel's body was buried, Grandma Charlotte

* *Avalasses* are brief torrential rains.

told me about the plans and dreams Ma Thérèse had had for her grandson. She had wanted him, a Creole slave child with small ears and large lips, a talented young man, to have a trade, to one day buy his freedom. She had already imagined him freed, with maybe one or two apprentices working under him. When he was barely six years old, she encouraged him to study the wigmaker and his assistants carefully who were summoned to groom Fayot. At that time he was an important white man with thick, ruddy hands, who had arrived accompanied by three slaves. Master Chantellec was content to supervise Negroes who did all the work: untangling, combing, ornamenting hair. From time to time he slapped them, hit them with a hairbrush, or gave them a kick. Samuel was always present at these hairstyling sessions with Monsieur Raoul and the master, and he confided in me that he liked neither wigs nor the bushy, often dirty hair hidden underneath them. Rather, my friend was fascinated with the tailor who would come by when the men tried on clothes. The thought of tailoring, cutting, and sewing together pieces of fabric to create a garment left Samuel feverish with excitement. One day, when I was barely nine years old, he made me a small, simple shirt with one sleeve longer than the other, but I thought it was marvelous. Samuel received fifteen lashes because he had not only stolen the seamstress's scissors but had also taken a bolt from beautiful pink cambric the mistress had planned on making into a bed jacket. My childhood friend died before he could become a hairstylist or a tailor; he died before he could become a man.

That day I asked my grandmother, "Grandma Charlotte, what dreams do you have for me?"

The answer came to me that night, while we lay on the bed side by side, emptying our heads intentionally to avoid hearing the prayers said in hushed voices, so as not to break the law on Negro burials, and to forget the cold shovelfuls of dirt that covered up a small boy with laughing eyes and dexterous hands. "I dreamt that one day your children's children would confront the barracoons, fly up into the sky, and write your name on the highest stars."

I rush toward Vincent without worrying about the galloping beats of my heart that blend with my confused fear. "By Gallifet spring, before the end of the day." I'll be there. I fly, and though my feet are sure and swift, my spirit falters. Yesterday Michaud seemed so tense and sad: "Be brave, Lisette. Vincent needs you. Be there before the first rays of the sun touch the topmost branch of the *mapou* tree."*

I'm already there. I fly, and my legs erase the four months of absence, the nights replete with nightmares suited only for latrines, where they can mix with the odor of the droppings from which they come. Four months of being startled by the slightest laughter fluttering across a pair of lips, by the slightest voice uttering a curse, by the slightest breath breathing misfortune. The time of smiles suspended by the possibility of bad news is finally over, the time of sighs and averted eyes has come to an end.

I had been ready for anything. When I see Vincent standing against the tree, my muscles relax, and I suddenly inhale the sweetness of the mountain. The wind's freshness glides

* A drought-resistant, sinuous tree native to the Caribbean region, often called a silk-cotton tree.

over me, bringing me relief, and I let it awaken all the sensations that refused to linger on my anguish-riddled flesh. I fly, light and full of desire from the thought of the sparks that will fly once more from his body to mine, when there is no longer any space between us.

I thought I was ready for anything, but my courage falters when I'm confronted by the horror. I stop myself midflight when Vincent turns around, and I see his profile away from the tree trunk. I see his eyes, thick beneath the undergrowth of his bushy brows; his face, ravaged by recent scars; his chest, noticeably thinner; his hips, whose slightest movements I know. My eyes travel down his powerful legs, which have walked and will walk a thousand times with me. My eyes see only one foot, the left one. He's raised his pants and the void captures my gaze and imprisons it. I see nothing but this empty space, and I tremble. How long did I stand there staring at it? Was I ever able to stop? I feel human again in Vincent's arms, and our shivering bodies meet. He murmurs words that find refuge in my hair and eyes. I drink our tears, and when we fall on the grass together, I am smothered. Our hands invent words that will never be repeated. Through his hands his rage explodes, lacerating my hot, tear-streaked skin and releasing me from the memory of all the horrors I'd accumulated during his absence. Using my body, his hands pantomime the story about the stump that is cut and dies. I hear it fall on the hard-packed earth, staining it red. In a painful reflex Vincent's hands push mine away as they persist in trying to touch the stump of his thigh that is haunting us. When I finally place my hand on it, I feel the scars, gathered into a bud that conceals the facts of their existence from me. I stroke them with small, hesitant caresses, exposing them, I brush them lightly with my arms, even my breasts, my thighs, my belly, and I am so filled with desire and rage I even rub my moist and wild sex savagely against them.

For once Vincent sets aside his usual good sense and the elaborate precautions he takes when we meet. He doesn't think of telling me to leave as his voice trails along the horrors that must be exorcised and the anguish that turns skin inside out. For the first time ever, Vincent tells me of the crossing on the ship, of feeling homesick from head to toe, of his arrival in Cap-Français. With the voice of an adult, sounding like the hoarse voice of a sad child, he tells me the story of the selling of bodies, of the death at sea of his father, who had been captured with him on the coast. The long, relentless tossing about of the slaves between sky and sea, the dead bodies thrown overboard, the chains, the pain of salt seeping through pores, the dull gaze of the slaves one doesn't dare see, for one has nothing to give them and too much to take. Does Vincent sense my most secret nightmares that rear up in the face of this ever-growing tragedy? I don't want to experience the days of living in the ship's hold, all of which is lodged in a terrorized and defiant child's body, a child who has come to understand that survival means being stronger than the pain. It means becoming strong enough that one can look away from the woman weeping for her dead infant, not see the man screaming under the lashes that slice, cutting his back. With his voice Vincent holds me tighter. We find ourselves wrapped around one another, nestled in our clumsy need for tenderness and dignity. Our desperate, feverish caresses are no longer enough, but we can't help ourselves.

Vincent tells me that when he arrived on the island, Paul-tre, from Plaisance, bought him and boasted afterward that he had appreciated Vincent's physical strength and intelligence immediately. So many *bossale* children were dying, unable to adapt to the dry tropical winds and illnesses that struck, one after another. A year after he arrived, Vincent had learned to speak French and serve a meal. Five years later he would take care of the master's horses and work as a footman, accompanying Paultre on the step of his stage-coach, learning to care for animals with the help of a mu-latto whose former master was a veterinarian. As an adolescent, Vincent healed wounds, drew blood, and soothed the horses' stomachaches, while his master was al-ready imagining the fivefold return on his original invest-ment. Feeling generous toward this slave, whom he expected would make him a nice profit, Paultre, showing his good nature, nicknamed Vincent "The Fearless One" because of his intrepid nature.

"It was then, when I saw that he was beating me as hard as he beat his animals, that I found freedom again. The horses' proud and mocking neighing and their long, shiv-ering tails challenged me to follow them. Paultre thought I was taming them, but actually I was following their rhythms, adapting to the demands of their animal dreams, their hostility to chains and paddocks. The day I left the plantation, I freed the most beautiful, the proudest horse of all. That is surely what Paultre holds against me the most."

Vincent holds onto one happy memory from childhood: a pair of soft, damp arms smelling of orange and lemon leaves. Babette, the washerwoman on the plantation, would put leaves in the laundry to make it smell of fresh air and sunlight. Armed with soapberry and lemon slices, Babette would attack both the dirty linen and the mournful odor of misery. Babette would bring that child with the angry face to her chest and make him eat a ripe mango, a piece of sugarcane, or a deeply salty yam and give him a smile or a caress on the cheek. And as a child, Vincent, despite having learned to erase the too-distant memories of a hand clasping his own, let Babette tame him with her scent of orange and lemon trees. Today, in my arms, as an adult Vincent weeps over the torture and the lashes Babette was subjected to when he ran away. Paultre had deemed the washerwoman guilty by association. What else could explain how a slave child planned his escape all by himself and managed to dodge the bloodhounds as well as the constabulary? Vincent learned of Babette's punishment months later, but his eyes tell me that it was on that day that he really came to know hatred. Today his desire for vengeance clouds his instincts and overtakes his drive. As he talks, I feel its presence in his amputated leg, whose knee, still unaccustomed to the void, swings and trembles.

When I get to the shack that night, Ma Augustine is waiting for me, lying down but with her eyes open.

"Lisette, it smells like danger, blood, and anger around here. You know just what I'm talking about. Don't wait until your life closes in on you to know what to do with it!"

I let my body fall down on the already cold floor and lay my head on my godmother's increasingly frail thighs. Somewhere in the deep recesses of my weariness, I know I should try to understand the wisdom she imparts to me, just like

Grandma Charlotte did before she died. But I can't linger tonight. I'm afraid of the hint of a good-bye that insinuates itself into her words. My youth longs for the calendas, the coral necklaces and images of sun-filled fields, where there are no bent backs, no overseers, no children dying. My youth wants to erase the stories of *The Infamous Rosalie* and barracoons, to lift off this weight that clouds my vision whenever I try to dream.

TYPICALLY, THE UNSPOKEN COMPLICITY between Gracieuse and I becomes apparent when we tidy the mistress's armoire. The scents of perfumed silk and lavender, the brushing of muslin, and the shimmer of colors send us into a blissful reverie. Sometimes, when we're feeling merry and malicious, we hold silk petticoats in front of us and swing our legs under them, imitating the elegance of Creole women. Our hips take on a languid cadence, our tightened buttocks draw out the subtle sway, and our feet seem to tremble at the touch of an invisible but unmistakable caress. We whirl around with open arms and smiles hidden beneath unsayable promises. Normally, we forget the slaps, insults, and humiliations, the clothes the masters throw at us when their merry whiff has worn off, when the colors of the rainbow are no longer visible, having long ago disappeared. We take a stroll down imaginary boulevards, indifferent to the mirror's fleeting reminders of the dull blue and white of our serge skirts, under our rustle of disguise.

Usually, my chatter irritates her, and sometimes in her disdain she hurls hurtful insults at me, not expecting any response. Then, satisfied at having brought her out of her impassivity, I happily spin on my heels and stick out my tongue. But today silk, taffeta, and rice powder cannot rouse my imagination. I feel Gracieuse's eyes on me, questioning my uncommon silence. I let this new lethargy slow down my gestures and curtail my words. I've already caught Ma Augustine's eyes peering at me as well, and I'm unable to assuage her concern. I would have to understand first what has been happening with me since my last visit with Vincent. It's as if in my confusion I become invisible in the midst of a swollen stream, as if I become a drop of water in the downpour of the cascade, not knowing whether to ripple or gush out, whether to fall or explode into a thousand wet and wounded bubbles. I ache, unable to tell the origin or the nature of what gnaws at me. My existence depends on me accepting my distress.

My rebellious spirit locks itself away. Gracieuse casts a mocking look my way. Standing before the mistress's mirror, she holds a light blue nightgown against her body that envelops her in soft, mysterious clouds. More than ever, her eyes hold their secrets while inquiring about mine.

"Why the long face?" she asks me casually. "One fewer leg doesn't mean your man is dead."

Stunned to realize that Gracieuse knows not only about my relationship with Vincent but also that he is a Maroon who was caught and punished, the growl of a rabid beast seizes me, and I watch Gracieuse recoil.

"Come now, calm down, it's for the best, my dolly. If the shades of your soul are so visible on your face, you are revealing your weapons and strength, and you'll lose your freedom."

I don't answer Gracieuse. My anger has subsided, and my confusion, in its tendency toward solitude, separates me from her and her world of cunning.

My days take on a dullish hue. I go, I come, turned toward the unfolding images and feelings that whirl inside of me. Ma Victor worries when she sees me eating without pleasure; Jeannine is surprised at my lack of responsiveness to her jokes and gossip.

The sniffling of a child finally pierces the shapeless clouds that envelop my being. I am suddenly brought back to the real world of sugarcane and whippings. I find myself near the shack belonging to Louise, little Mariette's mother. I see the girl collapsed by the single shut door nearby. She turns to me, and suddenly I feel her small body crash against mine. The sobs shaking her entire body from head to toe make my steps wobble. I remember hearing that Mariette's mother had just given birth. "All pink," Ma Augustine told me, "with eyes so blue we're afraid to look at them for too long, for fear we'll see through them. She's the lightest-skinned, the whitest of Louise's four children. She definitely got what she wanted this time."

Louise is a Nago woman, neither ugly nor beautiful, with wide-set ears and lips tightly sealed on her plans for light-skinned progeny. She had sworn to bring into this world only the children who had a chance to live without grinding their days in the cane fields. No one knows the identity of the father of Louise's firstborn: Zachary, with black curly hair and long eyelashes, his brown eyes speckled with gold. Zachary was sold at such an exorbitant price, the master couldn't keep from smiling—this man famous for not showing any emotion during these transactions. It must have been because Zachary had arrived like an unexpected gift, an unexpected surplus profit from this Negress who possessed neither talent nor any noteworthy trait and for whom he had paid less than a thousand pounds. After laying his eyes one day on little Zachary, who, still unaware of his market value, was frolicking naked in the rivers with the other young children, the master summoned his mother. From the workroom Louise was transferred to the big house and from then on was a laundress under Mam'zelle Jeanne's supervision.

Ma Augustine believes that Louise never revealed the name of Zachary's father; there was no doubt that the name of the white man or mulatto who impregnated Louise was not of interest to Fayot. The important thing was that Zachary be raised close to the big house so the master would never forget to show him to visitors, planters, and traders. So it was that a merchant from Nantes decided to buy the child and bring him back home with him so the boy could be his valet. Grandma Charlotte told me that already by the age of eight, Zachary's long eyelashes made men and women alike forget their sex and their age.

I don't remember Zachary, who was considerably older than Samuel and me, but I can clearly see the face of his younger sister Colette, her pink lips and fire-red hair. Is she really the daughter of the brother of Belin, the manager who visited the plantation twice? In any case Colette was sold when she was nine years old to a Creole woman from Saint-Marc who was looking for a beautiful cocotte for her daughter. I had overheard the master telling Madame that she could buy the three new dresses she had coveted and increase the order for nougat, truffles, and wine from the French suppliers.

Ma Augustine told me that Louise had insisted the master obtain from the buyer the promise of freedom for each child sold. Every time she talks to me about it, my godmother's chin trembles, an undeniable sign that she's trying to control her tears but can't stop them from forming inside.

"At moments like these, Lisette, I'm happy not to have had any other children but you. Because you, you're my child who came straight from life itself. Charlotte and I were your mother and father simultaneously. Your mother left us so fast. Before we even had time to weep for her, you were demanding our attention. So, you came to us from death and love, from nights in the ship's hold and from madness. You came to me, a pulsing ball of flesh, as if life knew that my womb couldn't give birth. You came to me also with the rebellious eyes of the island on which you were born, with Brigitte's irrepressible will to be proud and free— she who did not know you but who gave you so much."

With one glance Ma Augustine stopped the questions that always rush to my lips whenever my great-aunt Brigitte's name is mentioned. "No, don't ask me to talk about it until I'm ready, Lisette."

My godmother's fingers lingered on the locks that peeked out from under my scarf, and I leaned on her solid, dependable tenderness.

"It's true that for many years, while my lifeblood was still warm and fresh, I cried because I would never feel a baby growing inside of me. But over time, as I watched you grow, despite all the painful and perverse tricks mothers invent to protect their children, I wondered whether I would have had the courage to watch two beings I loved come of age. You see, Lisette, watching your children grow up on this island is to open yourself to so much misfortune, to hold your stomach so firmly it takes the layers of pain and accepts them with less indignity. It's always keeping an eye turned inward so misfortune doesn't take us by storm. It's praying, hoping, cursing, and often being afraid to smile. Sometimes I wonder what could be going on in Louise's head."

Like Ma Augustine, I often looked at Louise when she was carrying Mariette. We were all sure the child would be mixed, trusting Louise's ingenuity for choosing the father of her children. With café au lait color and long, thin black braids, Mariette was openly recognized by Béliard, who promised to buy her and free her when she turned fifteen. He might be able to do it, since he has friends on the High Council of the Cap! That's because I heard him say at the master's table that the law forbids whites from freeing children born of Negro or mulatto slave women, unless they marry the mother, and I can't imagine Béliard marrying Louise in order to free Mariette, even if he's still unmarried.

"Tell me, where would we go?" Villiers always asks. "These mixed-bloods already tend to consider themselves equal to whites. What's more, freeing them might cause all kinds of problems in the colony. Have you heard about the vendor from Bordeaux who married a Creole at home in France, a mixed woman, and had the audacity to return to Saint-Domingue with his beauty? In Port-au-Prince, if you please. Well, listen to this, Déracine, Negro-spoiler that you are. The honest citizens of the town complained, and Sir Genty and his mixed wife had to leave the colony. That would have been, you must agree, ladies and gentlemen, an awful precedent for all those whites thinking of officially coupling with Negresses. A few moments of pleasure, of course! But wanting to marry them is madness!"

At these moments the mistress always makes a snide comment to remind Villiers that they all know of his affair with Juliette, the *griffonne** he bought in Saint-Marc six years ago. In fact, she's the one who runs the Villiers house, since he isn't married. Fontilus told me that Villiers had nevertheless warned Juliette that if she ever became pregnant, he would not take care of the child. It seems that this *griffonne* is very tough on the other slaves in the big house and has them whipped for the most trivial things. Villiers gives her complete control but never mentions her at the masters' table. Yet he isn't embarrassed to accuse other whites taken with Negresses "of falling in with tafia and Negresses." Fontilus says that Villiers, on the other hand, has fallen in with the *griffonne* and that he wouldn't be surprised if one day he died from poisoning.

Curled against me, Mariette, Louise's little mulatta child, calms down, winding one of her braids around her finger.

"My little brother's going to die," she tells me.

Ma Augustine and Ma Victor, who had been helping Madeleine the midwife, made sure that she took all the necessary precautions. The door and the window had been closed to prevent the newborn from succumbing to a draft. They watched the midwife extract all the blood from the umbilical cord before cutting it from the navel. The child was swaddled in an obviously used, but clean and tidy, white

* A woman slave who is three quarters black and one quarter white.

woolen cloth. Meanwhile, despite all these precautions, the baby has been refusing to nurse for two days now. Yesterday I saw Ma Augustine and Ma Victor look at each other and shake their heads in discouragement, and I knew that the end was near. Newborns perish from trismus all the time. When they've survived a month, everyone breathes a sigh of relief, all the while preparing themselves for new dangers to come. Mothers battle worms, colic, and inexplicable fevers. Too often, death only delays its blow in order to strike us harder.

Here I am starting to think like Grandma Charlotte and Ma Augustine. Mariette raises her eyes the color of toasted almonds to me, expecting no response. I can only hold her against me and wait. She smells good, of orange leaves and lemongrass her mother puts in her bath. Her hair is washed and neatly braided. Louise has always taken good care of her children. One day I even heard Ma Victor teasing her about this. "You're lucky Fayot has lots of water, Louise. Otherwise, how could you bathe your children so often?"

Louise didn't answer. She isn't the kind of woman who likes to talk. I remember that she had just combed Colette's hair. She ran her hand through Colette's red hair then sniffed the freckled skin of Mariette, who was still a baby then, as if the Nago woman couldn't believe that these two small Creole children really belonged to her. It's as if she were already bidding them farewell.

Louise's scream pierced the walls of the closed shack, a seething cry of despair that nothing could contain. We both felt it in our gut and instinctively bent over to lessen its impact. Mariette began to sob. The sound of old women cries coming from this child's body claws at the indifference I've felt since seeing Vincent's amputated leg. A cool breeze jostles my uncertainty and drowsiness. I leave Mariette to hands from neighboring shacks that have come to gather up the suffering. The slave women make the most of every misfortune by opening the floodgates to the pain that constantly drains their will to live.

They arrive one after another, bringing with them the anxious distress of having to show up yet again. Amélie weeps for her oldest daughter, accused of witchcraft and arrested last month. Rose-Marie pulls her hair out for her husband, who ran away two months ago. She dreamed that he had been captured. Ma Thérèse appears as well, crying just like she did the first time, at Samuel's premature departure. Doubled over, Clara beats her chest because she's having a hard time living and already tried twice to kill herself. Is she crying because of her failed attempts or her weakness for still wanting to live?

I glimpse Ma Augustine and Ma Victor as they enter the shack to care for the pink corpse of the baby who will not fulfill his mother's dreams. I leave the tears and the moaning, the songs and the prayers. The master will no doubt allow the wake; he'll even send a gallon of brandy to soothe Louise's grief. But she should not abandon her plan to birth free children with bronze, pink, or tan skin! Louise's body can still bear at least two more children before no man—whether white, mulatto, quadroon, or octoroon—will want to touch it.

Here I am back in my favorite refuge for when I want to be alone without being too far from the plantation. Hidden again among the branches of the tree where I bury my treasures, I gently stroke my talisman. Can it protect me from the unease taking root in me? I caress my great-aunt Brigitte's cord, as if to beg her to tell me its secret.

Will Ma Augustine tell me on a day of great pain, like Grandma Charlotte had promised? I must learn not to pry secrets from the water that springs from the depths of the earth when and where it chooses. What if that water summons us to express our despair from time to time? What if it needs the impatience of our urgency?

Grandma Charlotte barely had time to tell me the story of the barracoons, which she had preciously kept to herself and for which she had prepared me for my entire childhood. She died two weeks after telling me.

"You'll need this wound to clear out the mist. You see, that way you will never forget this story. At moments like these, when life hurts more than usual, you'll know that light will come from the pain."

Grandma Charlotte was indeed right. My life today seems like a vast landscape where nothing is in its proper place—or do I have my head on backward? I'm in pain and still fighting so many mysteries that I can't tell my right hand from my left; I can't tell where to go or what to do. I feel this story invading me. I let myself be carried back to the time of the barracoons, which grandmother told me about, on a night of utterly familiar intimacy, a sweet night of braided hair and oily hands. I feel that I'll no longer be able to escape from the memories of that horror, these memories that have become my own. It's as if I were there with all of them: with Brigitte, tall and corpulent; with Charlotte, newly imbued with her body's beauty; with Augustine, shy and awkward; and with my mother, still too young to comprehend the ignominy of it all.

I was not expecting to hear the story that night. It was the end of a sweet, calm day, when Mademoiselle Sarah was still on the island. We had received no news of mutilated slaves or of aborted uprisings. It was a tranquil day, with a few unexplained blows, for a broken plate or a recently discovered theft. The mistress was in a good mood. She and Mademoiselle Sarah were inspecting their dresses, setting items aside and then casually throwing them away, guffawing when they came across especially outdated clothes. I was there, of course, picking things up and putting them away, wearing a willfully pleasant face to match the atmosphere I didn't want to spoil. Then suddenly, despite myself, my eyes fell on the dress I'd been coveting for so long.

As if under the spell of my strong desire, the longed-for words were spoken. "Sarah, why don't you give this dress to Lisette? You've gotten too tall to wear it for a while now. I wanted to offer it to your cousin Claire, but seeing how plump she is, I don't think it would fit her."

Mother and daughter smile with complicity at their mean-spirited words about poor Claire and at the confirmation of their own beauty that they implied. Meanwhile, I held my breath—would this blue percale dress with its long sleeves, high collar, and small bows of blue velour along the hem be mine? I didn't dare to breathe for fear of making a wrong move, a premature mistake. Sarah, with a brusque and malicious movement, pressed the dress against me.

"So, Lisette, you want it?"

"Here, take it, it will look better on you than on Claire in any case."

Then, as I held up my precious dress, she added offhand-edly, already focused on yet another frivolity: "You'll have to remove the lace from around the collar."

But nothing could dispel my joy that day. I thank her immediately with a proper smile and a slight bow. Instinctively, I contain my happiness to keep it from casting a shadow from its sheer force and magnitude. I control it, expressing just enough pleasure that the mistress and Mademoiselle Sarah can take satisfaction in their charitable act. Too much elation on my part could lead them to question the wisdom of their decision. It's the same as with adults who can't stand the tender, crystalline joy of children, threatening: "You're too happy today. I feel a spanking coming on."

As soon as I can, I run to show the dress to Grandma Charlotte and Ma Augustine. Their eyes meet over the saucepans, pots, and piles of vegetables wanting to be peeled. My unguarded joy shone on my face, and the apprehension I saw on theirs barely troubled me. In fact, I forgot about it altogether until that evening, when Grandma Charlotte beckoned me into the shack she then shared with Ma Augustine. That night I unwittingly found myself alone with my grandmother, and the seriousness in her eyes made me anxious.

"It's time I tell you about the barracoons, Lisette."

She said it in a voice that was sad and weary but filled with an unbending firmness, and a shudder went through me. Despite myself, my eyes asked her, "Why?" Grandma Charlotte's hand on my shoulder seemed to tell me to be patient and brave.

My grandmother's voice sounded different; no doubt it was my fear of what was about to happen that made her voice sound to me like the tolling of a bell. Grandma Charlotte began slowly and spoke without pause, as if she had chosen her words a long time ago.

"This whole story is like a vast wound. Some parts of it bleed more than others. There are more recent marks, not as fatal. Then there are old wounds that have stopped bleeding but have filled the entire body with a smell of rotting flesh. From time to time this stench rises to the surface with a whiff of decaying bodies, masking makeshift lies, baskets woven with happiness bought on credit. The time of the barracoons is a festering wound deep in the bones, a humiliation for all to see. When one has experienced this kind of humiliation, defeat can call your name at any time and undo your memory. My dear Lisette, I know you have your own wounds as well. I sometimes see the blood running through the songs you hum. I also know that you'll receive even deeper wounds and that surely, when that happens, I'll no longer be on this earth to help you temper the pain. No, my darling, you must not cry for what hasn't happened yet. Save your tears for the day I die. Listen to the story of the barracoons! Perhaps one day we'll no longer be talking about any of this. Perhaps one day we'll no longer even remember this word; it will have perished with those of us who bore its mark—but the shame will remain until we root it out. Our bodies will remain withered until we learn to take charge of our shadows and infuse them with life. I know that as a young Creole born on this island, so far from our land of origin, I know you've already seen and heard of a great many horrors.

"I've already told you about the slave ship, the ship's steerage, the ship's hold and the sea. There are some who found the days of the crossing to be the most horrible and painful. But for me the barracoons are the wound that will always bleed deep inside me. That was when I knew for sure that a large part of me had been buried. We all knew we had been packed into these camps to wait to be sold and taken to ships. The broker, a mixed man with gray-green eyes who wasn't any meaner than anyone else, had explained it to us! He had chosen to work as an intermediary between sellers and buyers. He traded us for barrels of tallow, Indian cloth, and all manner of silky, shiny, or sharp objects.

"The intermediary's name was Azor, and it was he who assigned us each a place in the barracoons. Men to the right, women to the left. Barracoons were camps surrounded by tall fencing under the surveillance of guards, white and black—we never noticed any difference in the threatening way they looked at us—and in our eyes the color of their skin blended with the harshness of their actions."

Grandma Charlotte spoke in a monotonous tone of voice, which was unusual, for she was always so incisive in her words and gestures. Her voice stung me, and sitting at her feet, I didn't dare to move. My eyes glanced at her face now and then, but I would quickly look away out of modesty in the face of this distress that preceded my birth.

"While we waited to board, we were held deep in a ditch surrounded by tree trunks, on top of which they had placed fallen branches. At dawn the guards led us toward large tubs of water in which to wash ourselves. They gave us enough to eat, even if some of us couldn't swallow the boiled rice drizzled with a spicy, peppery sauce. Sometimes we found pieces of goat meat in it. After all, we couldn't look too half-starved for the buyers! We even thought of throwing small limes in the water they served us. Sometimes they encouraged us to sing to keep our morale up, to forget our misery, to ease our fear. But inevitably, when night fell, we would hear wailing deep in the barracoons, screams of despair that made the big dogs, ready to rip apart our calves should we attempt to flee, growl. In any case who would have dared to do that with one's feet in chains? If the moaning had been especially doleful the night before, the guards would whip us randomly the next day, though always in moderation, so as not to mark our bodies before the sale was completed.

"I didn't count the number of days we spent there. My sister Brigitte, Augustine, who would become your god-mother, and Ayouba, my daughter, were next to me in the same barracoon, but believe me, my Lisette, I had never been so alone in my life. I saw Brigitte's anger in her long fingers that practically ripped apart the fabric we had been given to cover our most intimate body parts. Augustine pulled her skinny legs against her body in a protective gesture so childish it seemed indecent.

"I was paying attention to your mother: even the mother goat knows she must care for her young ones. I fed her when she refused to eat; I held her against me. I was no longer an Arada woman who had loved the sun and the sea. To me the barracoons represented the beginning of night, the end of liberty. The first captivity was the most ferocious one, the most irrevocable. Not even my body belonged to me. I no longer recognized it in my own mournful flesh. My spirit had left me, as if I were elsewhere, watching this spectacle from a distance. I seemed to be lost in the darkness in which I found myself.

"One day they brought us outside to stand in front of white men. I learned afterward that they were ship captains who had come from their ships that very morning with surgeons to inspect us. You know how it goes. Alas, you've witnessed the buying and selling of human beings since the day you were born. It's true you didn't feel those hands on your skin, rubbing it sometimes to see if it was really shiny or the product of lemon juice and gunpowder. No one forced open your lips to examine your teeth. No buyer ever spit in your face to make you understand that while there may have been physical closeness between you and him, there was no intimacy. But Lisette, you know how this can tear up the insides of a human being. Shortly after being inspected and purchased, we were branded. The surgeon was in charge, and he used red-hot branding irons made of silver. He smeared the top of my right breast with honey, then placed an oily sheet of paper over it before applying the seal. TR, the initials of the slave ship, the only letters I ever learned, were from the ship that brought me here. *The Rosalie*. Your eyes tell me that you would have wanted me to learn other letters, to understand the need to play with those forms, to use them and develop a complicit intimacy with them. For me it's too late: the alphabet will always embody the character of hell. The next day we were boarded onto *The Rosalie*. We left under cover of night. It seems that the slave traders normally lift anchor during the night to avoid the slaves' fierce attempts to return to their native land as they watch it slip from view. You've already heard the story of the crossing on *The Infamous Rosalie*. Today I wanted to tell you about the barracoons."

I wore the percale dress that I had dreamed of for so long only once. Then I went and tore it on a bramble, leaving it so pitiful that it elicited the reaction of Mademoiselle Sarah and the mistress I was hoping for: "Don't wear it anymore. It's sad to see such a beautiful dress in this state. You Negroes will never know how to appreciate beautiful things."

That day I received twenty lashes. My punishment was judged to warrant being carried out by the overseer himself. It was Michaud at that time, but I don't remember his face from then. While the lashes fell with sharp regularity on my naked back, I moaned and sobbed despite myself and could only hear Grandma Charlotte's voice full of unspoken reproaches deep within me. Beyond my tears I could only see the menacing abyss of the barracoons. For a whole week in the big house, they refused to talk to me, and my slightest gestures were met with slaps and rebukes. The other house slaves avoided me so as not to suffer the consequences of my downfall. Then the mistress and Mademoiselle Sarah grew tired of their dissatisfaction with me. After all, if they were always angry with me, what pleasure could they get from reminding me with a blow to the head or an insult from time to time that I was just a slave?

Grandma Charlotte was right. Deep in distress today, I summon my grandmother's last words the day she told me about the barracoons.

"Listen well, my dear Lisette. As we left the barracoons to board the ship, several of us were screaming. The captain called the interpreter over to calm us down. He explained to us at length with gestures that only fueled our fear that we were not going to be eaten by savage whites fond of flesh and blood, as many thought. He assured us that 'we were going to harvest the earth in a beautiful land.' In a way this was true. This island on which you were born is beautiful!

He could have added, without lying much more, that some of us would have beautiful clothes, *rassade* necklaces, shirts made of fine linen, taffeta dresses like yours . . ."

These words come back to remind me that I am a slave, and it is in this truth that my strength lies. Whether a field slave or a house slave, man, woman, or child, the slave is a creature who has lost his soul between the mill and the sugarcane, between the ship's hold and its steerage, between the crinoline and the slap in the face. Shame stains our every gesture. When we place our feet, undeserving of shoes, on the ground, when we let our exhausted bodies fall on cornhusk mattresses, and when we swing the bamboo fans, we crush our souls under the weight of our shame. Only our gestures of revolt truly belong to us.

TWO DAYS AGO MA AUGUSTINE LEARNED of the death of a new group of Negroes accused of poisonings. Since then my godmother expresses herself only by snarling because two of the fourteen killed were slaves who had come with her on *The Rosalie*: Charitable, a peddler; and OuganDaga, a Congo woman. They were shackled for two hours, then hanged in the public square.

"OuganDaga was renamed like all of us," Ma Augustine told me one day, "but I can't bring myself to call her Dada like everyone else does. For me she'll always be OuganDaga, just like an *ouanga nègess*, a bird too free to let her wings be clipped. The same thing happened with your mother. They renamed her Rose, but for us she was always Ayouba, full of the fragility of life that shone in her eyes and the softness of the wind couched in her steps."

Today Ma Augustine's sadness is heavy with the long list of the disappeared who have left her over the years: my great-aunt Brigitte, Grandma Charlotte, Ayouba, Tempête, Samuel, Amadis—the Ibo man she almost never talks about but who is there in the depths of her eyes those rare times I see her smile—and now Charitable and OuganDaga, her ship brother and sister.

Apparently, Charitable was accused and pleaded guilty to having used her position as peddler to take orders and distribute talismans, powders, drugs, and evil spells that OuganDaga supposedly concocted. Ma Augustine listened to the story of their interrogation, the confessions, the punishment meted out, and the execution that followed immediately afterward with pursed lips and tense hands. We all know what happens when a Negro accused of witchcraft and poisoning is questioned. Marie Grâce, the laundress on the Delerme plantation who was brought back from a long trip to Martinique, told us that the fear of poisoning is even stronger over there than it is here. Sometimes, she says, the accused are all stripped bare, their bodies are covered in sugar, and they are placed near an anthill until they confess. Over here they enjoy whipping them and burning them until they die or admit their guilt. Denunciations are encouraged, and the accused all mistrust each other.

It was the cook from the big house on the Fontaine plantation who denounced Ma Augustine's two friends. OuganDaga and Charitable were accused of having provided poison, verdigris, and other illicit drugs, as well as dangerous plants like the *Québec*, to dozens of slaves. It seems that a quadroon named Jeanne was the first to obtain these poisons to get rid of her mistress and marry Clergé, the father of her three children. Then several other slaves followed suit for all sorts of reasons, including Télémaque, who, to avoid coming under suspicion, eliminated his own entire family before killing his master.

While the coachman Pierrot, who's always up-to-date on everything, continues to tell the story, I remember hearing Charitable brag about her wares: "Come on now, ladies and gentlemen, have a look at these fruits and vegetables. I know you don't have yams anymore in your gardens, Ma Augustine. Just look at these avocados, Ma Victor—yours are certainly not ripe. Buy some fresh bread; the rivers are rising; the deliveryman won't be able to bring you any. Come on, Lisette, come closer, I have a special something for you: a fine, embroidered linen handkerchief. See how good it looks on you!"

No one could resist Charitable's enchanting voice—she would bring us into the intimate lives of all the town dwellers with juicy stories and would remind us of the names and the whereabouts of long gone, enslaved friends. Her litanies brought us closer to each other, beyond the plantation and the fields covered with sugarcane, beyond the hillsides awash in the changing colors of the cotton fields. Pierrot is the one who gave Ma Augustine news of OuganDaga since the two friends didn't see each other often, because the Fayot plantation was located in Margot. I know that during that time Ma Augustine had arranged a visit to the Congo woman and that OuganDaga herself had visited the Fayot plantation two or three times. Should I admit that she scared me a little? She had the habit of turning around suddenly and piercing you with her eyes, as if she were defying you. Imprisoned by her stare, I would feel so naked that my hands always grew damp.

On her last visit, less than a year ago, she said to me: "You'd think it was Brigitte who hadn't known the barracoons, a Brigitte from before the ship's hold and the branding. You're not branded, are you? You're a Creole! Not a *bossale* like Brigitte, Charlotte, Augustine, or me. You just have your Creole name, right? But we hold in our memory those names that sound the call for liberty: Ouda, Comba, Divia, OuganDaga. Lisette is just for you to put on, like a used dress they let you wear but that's not really yours."

Anger took hold of me completely, and I had a hard time containing the retorts that rose to my lips. The only thing that held me back was the respect I owed to Ma Augustine's ship sisters, but I gave her a stormy look. Then OuganDaga let out a victorious laugh, and stupefied, still furious, I watched the trace of a smile cross Ma Augustine's face.

"Yes," my godmother's friend said after she calmed down. "Brigitte is certainly in that girl, that's for sure, my sister."

How I wanted to take Ma Augustine's pain, older than my own, and put it in my collection of calamities, to erase the bitterness that seemed to permanently crease her lips!

That morning, having finally broken her silence, she sent me to the workroom on the Fontaine plantation to send a message to Marie-Pierre, another ship sister. Ma Augustine wanted Marie-Pierre to know about the deaths of Charitable and OuganDaga as soon as possible. Even in Grandma Charlotte's time, my godmother was always the go-between between the ship brothers and sisters.

Every time I have to go near the workrooms, I hurry by so as not to stay a minute longer than necessary. But today maybe it's the memory of OuganDaga's laugh that makes my legs stop near the dark, smelly alleyways, and my ears pick up the echo of the songs the overseer and manager make the Negroes sing to keep them from falling asleep by the boiling furnaces and cauldrons. It's almost time for the break, and I stand where I can easily find Marie-Pierre among the dozens of slaves leaving the workrooms. The

Fontaine plantation is smaller than Fayot's, but it still has eighty-four slaves working in the workrooms and the fields. I don't dare to look directly at the figures marching by me: their underwear, made of thick fabric, torn here and there; their skirts, made to spare as much fabric as possible, barely covering the women's bottoms. Fontaine is not quite as cheap as the others, who let their slaves go about without shirts and with just a bit of cloth to cover their genitals, but as they say at the master's table, it looks like things aren't flourishing for some planters. Fontilus, on the other hand, says that the only reason whites dress and feed slaves is that if they didn't, their cotton, indigo, and sugarcane plantations wouldn't yield much. Otherwise, they'd let us starve to death, dirty and naked. I try to hide my serge skirt and blue shirt behind some trees, while the group of raggedly dressed slaves passes nearby. But few of them notice me; several have turned their eyes inward, toward hell. I want to flee this place, but despite myself, the sound of their steps pins me where I stand. Heavy and desperate, they press down on the earth with the weight of their suppressed sobs.

Suddenly Marie-Pierre, who spotted me before I saw her, places her hand on my arm. A Congo woman like Ougan-Daga, Marie-Pierre seems an extension of the earth itself, with her small body, and her skin, a cracked reddish mountain hue. She smells of sugarcane since she spends her whole life pushing cane stalks through the rollers. Ma Augustine is afraid that one day she'll hear that her friend got her hand caught in them: in such cases the manager has the arm cut off immediately with one strike of a billhook. Sometimes the slave doesn't survive the infection that spreads throughout his body. This of course explains Ma Augustine's particular affection for Marie-Pierre. Today she has charged me with the mission of giving her leaves for tea and oil for massages. Yet I wonder if all Brigitte's legendary knowledge, combined with the wisdom of Grandma Charlotte, Ma Augustine, and OuganDaga, can relieve the pain that bends Marie-Pierre's back and soothe the burns that deform her fingers. What could wash the stain of filthy ashes from her gaze? Marie-Pierre's long, streaked face clears slightly under Ma Augustine's loving, attentive care; her hands linger on the cinnamon cookies, the bits of gingerroot for the nighttime tea, the leaves of soursop, basil, and mint. By the time I find the courage to tell her of the deaths of OuganDaga and Charitable, Marie-Pierre has already finished her gourd filled with rice soaked in sauce. She lowers her head further, as if she were sinking a little more into the earth.

"I was expecting bad news because of the nightmare I had last night. You'll tell Augustine for me that last night I returned to *The Infamous Rosalie*. I didn't want to go; the steerage was filled with people battling a terrible storm. I wanted to save myself, so I tried to throw myself into the waters to escape the arms that were clutching me from all directions. But you know how dreams can be dishonest and can put you through hell and high water. Suddenly I found myself lying on the floor, in the darkness of the barracoons, chained to dogs that were giving birth. Totally black, brawling pups were coming out of their wombs. Lisette, I admit I was terrified. Then I saw Brigitte in my dream, as magnificent as always, still tall and beautiful, but with tears in her eyes. I never saw your great-aunt cry, even when one of the whites punched her directly in the chest, even when they locked her up alone in a little cubbyhole, where she had to stay bent in half, barely able to move. But in my dream I saw her cry. Her tears fell in thick, violent torrents. Several slaves were screaming as they passed through the waters, and I begged Brigitte to stop her tears because we were all going to drown if she kept on crying. Then we turned around in the steerage; the waters were falling on us, sousing the ship. It looked like we were all going to perish. That is the bad faith of nightmares: they enjoy playing tricks on our minds. Then I screamed too and woke up drenched in sweat. I feel like I left the dream too soon and missed the end of it!"

Marie-Pierre held my thighs for support as she got up. The tumult of the dream had already left her eyes, and her body regained the posture of a slave who is prisoner to bundles of cane. She seems to shut down her senses to keep from feeling anything other than the smell of the sugarcane alcohol that saturates her, but she makes a final, insistent gesture toward me: "Be sure to tell Ma Augustine that I saw Brigitte cry."

Then she returns to the workrooms. I didn't have time to ask her to talk to me about my great-aunt, she who haunts the dreams of those who knew her . . .

Once again, my questions remain unanswered.

I have to find Michaud to receive a message from Vincent. I'm a little worried. Since his leg was cut off, my man has become more determined than ever to remain free. He's thinking of going west, where it will be easier for him to pass unnoticed by the constabulary, who doesn't know who he is, and to make contact with other Maroons.

"My Lisette," Vincent said to me at our last meeting, "we

mustn't forget that this island has its own four ends of the earth. Ants take their time to cross the road, but one day they reach the other side."

These profound words leave me with even more distress. Grandma Charlotte, Ma Augustine, Ma Victor, Michaud, Vincent, and even Gracieuse the cocotte seem to have their heads in the clouds. They're all talking about a soon-to-be-solved mystery, as if I should be learning to suss out the secret of words and dreams to find the hidden truth inside! All the while, deep within me, I feel the pitter-patter of life like an old song whose music suddenly breaks off after the first chords.

Yesterday, while we were cleaning the masters' room from top to bottom, Gracieuse was acting rather strange. Although she rarely pays attention to anyone else, she kept casting pensive looks at me. It seemed as if she had a question poised on the tip of her tongue, one that she hesitated to ask, leaving it dangling on the edge of a precipice. Gracieuse, dear cocotte, who defies life with every sway of your hip, with each brush of your insolent gaze, I don't recognize you in this young woman with her distressed and clumsy gestures.

As soon as I see Michaud's face, I know that Vincent has left and that I will have to get accustomed to a new kind of absence. This one will be more painful than being apart from him for months at a time; it will be like a void without any hope of seeing him pop out suddenly from behind a tree, without the tender illusion of imagining him in some familiar place. His will be a double absence: far from my eyes and from all familiar landscapes. I'll have to learn to make the four ends of the earth disappear to find him again. How I fear the despair that awaits me! Michaud tells me to sit down with a gesture of his remaining arm. Mist is already enveloping the distant hills, and I wrap the tail of an old scarf around my shoulders. But it isn't the cold that makes my lips quiver.

"No one can stop the fog, Lisette. It glides everywhere, even when we don't see it at first; it clings to the leaves, the trees, the stones, the boulders, the hills. When you think you've gotten the best of it, you realize that it has completely enveloped you. One finds oneself its prisoner, unable to move forward. It's the same for freedom. It makes its own way, and no one can stop it. Your man is like a small fog, a miniscule patch that fastens onto others to form an invincible mass. I think you could have changed his mind, my Lisette, but one day he would be angry with you for doing so, for no one—not even you—can quench his thirst for freedom he carries inside."

"I love the freedom that exists in him, you know it, Michaud!"

But my voice's echo reaches me full of tears and doubts.

I feel so distraught after leaving Michaud that it seems to take me twice as long to reach the plantation. Standing by the kitchen, Ma Victor gestures strenuously for me to follow her. One after the other we arrive at the house she shares with Gracieuse. I have no time to ask questions since she's in a great rush; I could have caught up with her, but the sorrow has just begun to settle in me, and my legs are heavy. It's not the first time that I've entered Gracieuse's place. She's made a desperate attempt to dress up misery. Old pieces of slips in a variety of colors are plastered on the only window. On what serves as her bed, she has thrown a mended rug, decorated with flowers. Despite it all, it's just a Negro's shack like any other. It's a prison cell like any other, where life will never be as it should.

I see Ma Augustine and Madeleine, the midwife, standing around Gracieuse's bed, surrounded by clumps of old rags stained red. The camphorated oil and infusions fill the air with the smell of incurable disease.

"What's happening, Ma Augustine?"

But my questions dry up the instant I see Gracieuse's face in the bed where she's lying. Looking stiff and drained of blood, her face reminds me of those wax dolls the mistress enjoyed collecting one year until she grew tired of them and sold them to the Delerme family. Like them, Gracieuse's two open eyes seem to stare into space.

"Gracieuse."

Without thinking, I take her fine, small hands between my own. So cold. She turns her face toward me, and for one delicious second, full of all that could have been, nostalgic for all that existed before, I find her ironic smile.

"So, little one, as you can see, I lost the round this time. That's life."

Her voice is nothing but a breath, but her words reach me, brutal and clear.

"Take good care of yourself. Don't trust anyone. There's an evil eye in the big house."

Then her eyelids slowly close. I feel life leaving her fingers. Confusion overtakes me. It's not the first time I see someone die before my eyes. For a slave death is a daily part of life. One waits for it at every corner of the road, but one never gets used to it. Every time I see a living person pass over to the beyond in the blink of an eye and watch the person take off in a flutter of eyelashes, I am overtaken by a feeling of powerlessness, a sensation of emptiness like a waterfall whose waters fall nowhere. Ma Augustine presses me against her body, my face resting on her frail thighs. My tears fall on her white skirt, washed so many times, while her words enter me, scraping away at my pain and remorse.

"Cry, my Lisette, because we should cry for our dead, but know that Gracieuse chose her fate. The Fayot's cocotte was not a naive woman, and she hated slavery. She refused to give birth to children who would have been slaves like she was, whether house slaves or not, cocottes or not. She made her body bleed seven times in a row. She had seven abortions secretly, without resting, except for one time when I announced that she had the measles. Since it was contagious and Mademoiselle Sarah was still here, Gracieuse was allowed to stay in bed for a week. I don't know if the master suspected anything, but the poor girl was bleeding so profusely and looked so sick that he feared for her life and preferred—or pretended—to believe me. All the other times Gracieuse went back before she was ready, her legs weak, her face pale under layers of powder. I think that Fayot suspected that his cocotte was having abortions, but he was never sure. In fact, she didn't want to bear children for any man, but especially not for Fayot or for any other white man. "No black children, no mulatto children. Chains have no color," she told me one day. Seven times she watched her blood flow; seven times I watched her body protest the abuse and call out for mercy. Madeleine warned her that the next time could be the last time. She tried not to get pregnant, but Fayot wanted to have a child by Gracieuse so badly that he watched her and forced himself on her at the fateful times of the month. They were waging a silent war, undeclared but tenacious and unrelenting. Two implacable foes! Did you know that Gracieuse came here when she was nine years old, yet one would have thought she was a Creole! She used her body to stay out of the cane fields and away from the cauldrons of boiling sugar. She chose her hell. Is one hell better or worse than another? Yes, I know you never suspected a thing. She didn't want me to tell you. She liked you a lot, you know."

I liked her too. Those words never pass my lips, for their profound truth just now reveals itself to me, wreaking havoc. I will no longer see the cocotte elegantly arching her slim waist. I will no longer see her pouting, quivering lips. One more absence to add to the void. I now remember seeing Gracieuse's hands caress her belly, a gesture of supplication and heartbreak that I hadn't understood. I cry for the friendship that could have existed between us. Her final message adds to my sorrow. What threat did she wish to warn me about? What danger lurks in the big house?

In the days afterward I have no time to revisit my sorrow. A new frenzy inhabits my steps. Fayot, seized by a cruel, cold rage, after learning of Gracieuse's death, decided to interrogate all the house slaves. Me in particular. Whip in hand, he rained blows and questions down on me without ever losing his composure, patiently awaiting my answers. My body, streaked with red, meets the whip that has cut through the fabric of my skirt and is savagely lashing my skin. But what could have I told Fayot? That his young and beautiful cocotte preferred to die rather than to bear his child? That she chose to kill her own children seven times to keep them from being slaves like her? It's not for me to divulge Gracieuse's secret to the man I consider responsible for her death. In the face of Fayot's frustration and anger, I forget the biting lashes on my flesh. I join Gracieuse, proud to have chosen my own hell too.

My memories of Vincent and Gracieuse mingle in me as if they shared the same voice, the same breath. Their departure heightens my confusion, creating an enormous void in my life. These two people, who had never known one another, are joined within me!

Although Ma Augustine doesn't ask me any questions, I sense her worry in her insistent gaze, in the weight of her hand on my hair. But my secret doesn't belong to me, and I have no right to put my godmother in danger by revealing my activities. On top of it, Michaud requested my absolute silence for everyone's sake. It's my job to report to the families of Maroons news from their husbands, brothers, sisters, mothers, daughters, or friends. Good or bad news, from the Fayot plantation or another plantation in the area, I have to figure out how to keep them informed. Since Gracieuse's death and Vincent's departure, I am the intermediary between Michaud and the families of Maroons. Sometimes I also pass on rather complicated instructions, when Maroons want a family member to join them in the hills.

"In a week get your machetes and provisions ready."

"I'll come by to see you in a month. Leave the provisions near the storehouse."

At first the slaves eye me suspiciously, but soon after, when they see me coming, the ones with Maroons in their family expect me to bring them little tidbits, a word, a hope, a whiff of news. When I have nothing to tell them, I watch their eyes go back to looking like murky water, opaque and somber. When night falls and I'm tired from my errands, I lie down next to Ma Augustine and immediately fall asleep. I know my godmother will wake me before dawn so we can return to the big house. My job is to tidy up and clean the masters' bedroom, with Mariette and Joséphine's help of course. The cocotte's place seems to have been bequeathed to Jeannine. She takes care of the mistress's petty desires and whims, fetches her nightgown, handles the fan, covers her with her shawl. I try to be as diligent as always to avoid all criticism, especially since Fayot has put me under strict surveillance. From time to time his face darkens, and he looks at me with great mistrust.

"Don't forget Gracieuse's last words," Ma Augustine tells me often when she sees me rushing over to the big house, my eyes sparking with fire. Without ever answering her directly, I heed her advice and strive to present to everyone the reassuring image of a happy, smiling Lisette. Yet when I look at myself in the mirror, whether in the small broken mirror piece that Grandma Charlotte gave me or in the big, oval mirror in the mahogany frame on Madame's dressing table, I find that I can't quite recognize myself. My enormous, worried eyes fill up the space, and I back away at the sight of their fire. My nostrils quiver by themselves, as if I no longer had control over them, and my lips are parted, eager and impatient.

Do I manage to hide this face from the people around me, especially from the evil eye Gracieuse warned me about? Should I suspect these familiar faces, people with whom I've shared beatings, humiliating insults, and despair? I can't bring myself to believe that Madeleine, the midwife who did everything she could to save Gracieuse, or Ma Victor would want to hurt me! Should I mistrust Louise and Clarisse, Mam'zelle Jeanne or Rose-Marie? Despite myself, I glance furtively at Florville and at Jeannine, whose loud laughter sounds increasingly triumphant. Pierrot the coachman's constant gossip makes me suspicious of him. What might he have said about me? Fontilus's words stick in my mind: "With Pierrot the coachman, news spreads before one can even close one's mouth!"

I have no one to share my anxiety with. These days Ma Augustine seems so sad and vulnerable. I have no desire to fuel her fear. Without question I could have confided in my friend Fontilus. In an instant he would have made my fears disappear, and together we would have laughed it off. Alas! The time when Fontilus joked and pulled my hair and my skirts is over. The other day, without our ever saying a word, we ran into each other, and our suffering met as well. We stood there a long while, letting our despair flow from one to another. Then my friend from the calendas pushed me gently, with an old, tired gesture that made me keep going despite myself, backing away without taking my eyes off him, as though I wanted to keep the imprint of his hand on my hip forever.

More than ever, I mind what the masters say, noticing their anger, their rising fear, their rage at anything that could be a danger to them. I duly bring to Michaud information gleaned from dinners and words exchanged over drinks. Before it becomes official, I tell about the judicial decree stating that poisons and their antidotes must be tested on condemned poisoners. I talk about the planters' concern about the quality and price of products imported from France. I tell about Villiers's intolerance for absentee colonists, "those naive, lazy men who think they can supervise a sugar plantation in Saint-Domingue while living in Paris."

Without letting my face betray my thoughts, I follow the slightest word that the masters and their friends say to each other. As long as I fill each glass, set down and remove the plates, make little Manon—still trapped in her job of poison taster—try the food, the masters don't see me. Invisible to their eyes, I spy on them as efficiently as I serve them. In fact, all the slaves in the big house have learned the art of gathering information like I have. We know instinctively that we must pay attention to what the masters do and say to keep from making mistakes, to maneuver into a better position. Just to survive.

Since I started working with Michaud, I listen more carefully when I'm in the big house. And when I hear Villiers make an even more deafening entrance than usual, screaming: "Fayot! Fayot! Come hear the news, my friend!" I rush over. I, who usually keeps my eyes off Villiers, whose hands are always in search of a rear end to pinch, I find an excuse to get closer. As I expected, Fayot asks me to serve them a drink at once. A familiar name makes its way back into their conversation, while the mistress, who'd been putting on her make-up and perfume, joins them. I wonder how I can continue taking out the carafe and glasses in my shock at what I'm hearing. The news strikes me with a savage blow. They captured Makandal. My eyes sting, while my sure and reliable hands mechanically continue serving. Despite the fog that is settling in me, I collect the information pell-mell. At the Dufresne plantation. In Limbé. During a calenda. My heart skips, and my feet barely keep from betraying my feeling of helplessness. Knowing that Makandal was there, the whites let the tafia flow. The Negroes all got drunk, and Makandal's defenses were low. Nevertheless, he attempted to flee . . .

A flash shoots through me from head to toe. Did my anxiety lower my defenses? I try to assess the damage. No, I'm protected by my years of subterfuge. My days of diverting my tears from their rightful place have honed my skills in lowering my head and smiling submissively. Not one drop of wine on the tray, not one jingle of the glasses. My hand doesn't even tremble when Villiers adds with a big smile, as he pinches my rear end: "But the dogs caught him, and he was brought to the Council last Tuesday. The investigation is open."

I have only one thought: to find Michaud and bring him up to date, in case he hasn't already heard. But I must avoid hasty and careless actions at all costs. Negroes and Negresses will be punished and tortured if Fayot suspects they are in touch with Maroons, not to mention what Fayot would do to someone like me, the go-between. I keep my impatience and temperature in check so as not to force things, and I wait for the right moment to make my move. In the following days the masters and their friends organize parties and festivities, proclaiming loud and clear their joy at having rid themselves of "that barbaric savage and murderer." I won't be able to see Michaud until Sunday.

With plodding steps I reach the carriage house, with the full knowledge of Makandal's death inhabiting my body. I know Michaud has visitors, for he suddenly emerges from a corner of the building. His face seems to have grown older by ten years. He extends his right arm to me, and in no time we're supporting each other. Michaud leads me to the rear of the old shack, where he lives along with the other discarded people, on this small piece of land where, with old Désirée and the other survivors, he's planted a few fruit trees. Scattered under the shade of the orange trees, away from inquisitive glances, are gathered about twenty slaves. I see Rose-Marie with her grumpy face and Mam'zelle Jeanne from the big house, then several slaves from the workrooms, like Marie-Pierre and Roselène. Others came from plantations nearby. There are two or three people I don't recognize, who are probably Maroons, standing as close as they can to the tree trunks to make themselves invisible. I respond to their greetings with a nod of my head before sitting down at Michaud's invitation. We wait for Zamor, a Maroon who was present at Makandal's execution, to arrive. He promised Michaud he would give a report. There are no superfluous words between us. We're conserving what anguish we have left, holding it in suspense. Suddenly all heads turn toward the Negro whose multicolored clothes I spot first. That must be Zamor. When did he slip in among us? With graying, long, dry temples, he stands against a tree, a staff in his hand. His eyes are turned toward the hills, but his profile exudes such intensity that no one dares to move. Our apprehension fills the silence. Like all the others, I'm afraid of what this man will tell us. "It's true that he's dead," he announces finally, and our breath is released and floats above us. We're overcome with emotion, and our focus shifts to what he's saying.

"He was led to the public square. The whites wanted the Negroes to watch him burn. I was a few kilometers away when I heard the news, but I had to witness the execution. Up until the last minute I too was hoping he'd escape. Me, I don't believe in witches," Zamor added and spit on the ground. "But if a slave has a force within him that can help him crush whites, I won't try to take it away from him. I wanted to see with my two own *bossale* eyes, which had never learned to scorn the sun's warmth or the cries of birds. I understood long ago that life here could be born only in blood. I wanted to see if this Maroon—*bossale* and wild like me, one-armed like you, Michaud—was really going to die. When I reached the square, I slipped in among the crowd of slaves gathered before the main doors of the church, and I saw him. Bare chested, bound to a post, he held a torch made of wax. You should see the way his neck stuck out from the plank to which his body, his chest, and his back were bound. There was a kind of placard on which something had been written. I couldn't get close enough to read it, but I heard people say that they had written on it the crimes he had committed.

"'Poisoner': everyone knew it, he never hid that this was his dream and that he had poisoned a great number of people.

"'Profaner': because he had used "saintly objects" for his evil doings. I don't know about you, but the *bossale* Negro I am never understood the difference between saintly things and profane ones! I'm not one of these Negroes who considers a brother a "bush Negro" because a white priest hasn't sprinkled water on his forehead. Witches and priests both need so much fuss for their ceremonies! Whites must have known of other crimes Makandal supposedly had committed, but in my opinion a single one would have sufficed for him to be judged, condemned, and executed—for the simple fact that he had declared his opposition to whites and to slavery."

Zamor holds his tongue to let his words make their way into each of us.

"It seemed to me that they took a long time before they set the fagots of wood on fire. And yet I'm used to waiting. I'm used to waiting, without making a sound and without hurrying, for the moon to be exactly between two trees and under a cloud, before I move. I'm used to waiting as long as it takes, for it does no good to entice the wind and the sun to tell you the time. But standing there with nothing to do, waiting for them to burn him, time seemed to drag. That's always the case when we are powerless and helpless."

Zamor's gaze leaves this peaceful courtyard where the smell of orange and lemon trees seems to mock our somber silence and soar over this smoke-filled place. It seems that the smell of Paladin's burned flesh is mixing with Makandal's and that we're all slowly burning.

"When they set the fagots of wood on fire, Makandal began to howl. A cry of pain but also a cry of rage and revolt—an extraordinarily powerful cry. It's strange, but seeing him bound to the post, I felt the strength in him that made men, white and black, fear him so. Makandal tried to free himself from his chains. He struggled, kicked his legs, and shook his head like a madman. The crowd was screaming with him, when suddenly we heard a howl worse than all the others. The one-armed man had rushed out of the fire."

"It was true, then!" mutters Roselène. "He couldn't be burned."

"Quiet, woman!" Zamor shouts, as he strikes his staff against the ground.

He finally seems to have lost his cool and has to pull himself together before he can continue.

"Like you, the Negroes and Negresses present at the execution thought Makandal was going to escape, that he was stronger than that. Even the jailer Massé, who wouldn't hesitate to crush a Negro's skull with a staff, panicked when Makandal rushed out of the fire. You should have seen him trying to unsheath his weapon as he screamed, "Kill him, kill him!" The poor slaves who were there began to exclaim with joy. Their triumphant cries of "Makandal escaped! Makandal escaped!" burst forth without restraint.

"Then I saw another white man, perhaps one of the judges from the court, hold Massé's hand as he was about to kill Makandal with a thrust of his sword. They caught the one-armed man and bound him to a plank. They put him back in the fire, in front of all the slaves standing there."

"This time Makandal did not rush out of the fire. I saw him burn. The white man from the court turned to the crowd and loudly proclaimed: "You see, Makandal is dead. We burned him, and he did not turn into a mosquito. He is dead. Makandal is dead."

Zamor turns to Roselène and adds with a voice so muffled it resounds in us like a pummeling fist. "Makandal is really dead." It's only when Roselène, distraught, begins to dry her tears that I realize that even before the story ended, many of us were shedding tears like drops of soundless rain.

THE SCREAMS REACHED THE BIG HOUSE around two in the afternoon. The masters were still taking their nap. We were finishing our cleaning, dishwashing, and gossiping. The rustling sounds of our voices were subsiding as if weighed down by the afternoon's languor.

The outcry startled us, making us jump. From her bedroom the irritated mistress sent little Mariette to find out what the ruckus was all about.

"It's impossible to get any rest around here! There's always some noise for no reason whatsoever!"

By then we were already outside, heading toward tragedy. I was running like the others, instinctively following those ahead of me but alarmed to see the direction they were taking. Among the slaves gathered in the distance, I recognized Pierrot the coachman, whose shack was near Fontilus and his father's shack. We approached the scream. There were raw sobs in the voice we heard, a blood-curdling sound. When we heard it the second time, it was less loud in its rage, as if reality had put an end to all hope.

Since Vincent's leg was cut off, I move through life taking small steps; I mistrust life and its unpleasant surprises. Since Vincent's leg was cut off, I conjure up my fears, commanding them to reveal themselves so I can smash them into a thousand maddening sparks. That's why, before I hear Fontilus's father let out another cry, I knew that my friend from the calendas had left too. I head toward the misfortune that awaits me with the rhythm of my moans as my only music.

Standing next to me, Florville holds me back to keep me from seeing the body. A few slaves had already gathered around the corpse. Pierrot the coachman and Charlemagne, a *bossale* who took care of the horses on the plantation, was holding Gentilus up. Fontilus's father was no longer crying, but he had shrunk so much that we could only see the top of his coarse, gray hair. They had laid Fontilus's body on the ground, but no one thought of taking down the rope that was still swinging between the tree branches with its grotesque, pitiful knot. The other slaves were hiding his body from me, of which I could see only a small part of his right leg beneath the cloth pants and his clean, bare feet—as if my friend from the calendas and Sunday parties had taken a bath and carefully washed up before telling life to *fuck off*.

My tears remained frozen inside me. The March night fog that makes bones frail and fearful had wrapped its coldness around my heart.

How can we feel both alive and imprisoned in the kingdom of the dead, unhappy and eager to live, lost in the darkness of despair and aware of each ray of light? A week has gone by since we found the lifeless body of Fontilus high in the sapota tree that is older than both our lives put together, as Ma Victor would often say. My friend from the wild dances will no longer be around to make Ma Victor's soft, full chest startle needlessly. "Calm down there, young man." He will never be around to tickle little Mariette and make her delicate laugh bubble forth, nor will he be around to make Clarisse run from his playful embrace.

I have to learn to live without him, without the gentle, flirtatious wind that always brushed my senses when Fontilus danced with me, no longer breathe the fresh, reliable air of our friendship that made us smile, just like that, for no reason at all.

I feel as if I no longer have any tears to shed. From Samuel to Grandma Charlotte, from Gracieuse to Fontilus, from Vincent to Makandal, from start to finish my sorrows have taken on the shape of an abyss that makes jumping into it so tempting. I've gotten into the habit of going to sit in the branches of the sapota tree after working in the big house and getting Michaud's messages, even though my whole body cries out for rest. It's as if the branches of the sapota still hold the imprint of my friend's neck, as if the wind rustling the leaves is the same one that last caressed his cheek. When I visit this tree, Michaud in his subtle way tries to follow my thoughts and fears. But how could I express the thicket of confusion that's inside me? In the big house they're all whispering about how Fontilus or Gracieuse want to take me with them, how my dead ones are actively seeking me, and how I'm already halfway gone with them.

For the first time I watch Ma Augustine lose the wonderful self-confidence that I also saw in Grandma Charlotte. My godmother called first on Ma Victor, then on Madeleine— who are both supposed to know all about roots and prayers.

Often I see their graying heads coming together, murmuring incantations. And yet, even as my legs dangle and I let myself be carried away by drowsiness, my senses vigorously remind me that I am alive. The moon's rays play hide-and-seek on my skin and hands, gliding up the length of my arms to reach my cool, soft shoulders. I tremble at the thought of the misfortunes to come, but my inane desire to see the sun rise every day always gets the better of my fear. Life is at my fingertips.

So many moments of my life were spent around the masters' table, serving guests, playing the role of the young domestic with docile eyes turned toward hell! It's fitting that life brings me back to their living room, while I place a dish for the umpteenth time on the damask tablecloth.

Since Fontilus's suicide, Manon has been released from her duties of poison taster, though this did not cause the terror-filled atmosphere to disappear. I had thought that with Makandal's execution, the panic would disappear in the north of the Big Island. After all, hadn't they burned the one-armed man in front of a crowd of slaves twelve miles from the city of Cap? Had they not confirmed that he was the leader, the one who trained slaves to murder their masters? Wasn't he the one whose ultimate goal was to annihilate all the whites on Saint-Domingue?

And yet the great fear is still present, and it even seems to have spread. Makandal's death seems to have whipped up a wind of panic and revived people's accusatory, vengeful instincts. Slaves are denouncing one another, executions are continuing at a crazy pace. There are now more than eighty slaves being held on charges of poisoning in the Cap's prison. Whites are more afraid than before, as if the death of the one-armed man had only been a respite, after which the threats of poisonings continued to loom large.

That night, though the feeling of being elsewhere slowed down my thoughts, I was listening to their conversation as usual: Madame simpering, always playing the role of the fragile, frivolous woman in front of the master's friends; Madame Déracine whimpering with a voice that turns every piece of news into a lamentation. I feel the anxiety filling Lescailles's words, he who, after five years in Saint-Domingue, can't make ends meet. Up to his neck in debt, as Belin the manager says, Lescailles doesn't know what advice to follow. Should he increase his sugar production to bolster his revenue? In that case he'll have to buy more slaves, which would mean going into more debt. This dilemma makes Lescailles impossible to put up with, according to Madame.

"Come on, dear, you're boring us! Don't start again with your woeful tales of debt!"

And so the nights pass steeped in the vile monotony of words and people. On that night it's Villiers's statement that draws my attention.

"I invite you to a show tomorrow night in front of the big house," he announces in a conspiratorial tone.

I see the Déracines' faces tense with apprehension. Lescailles studies his neighbors around the table, trying to detect some indication that would allow him to understand Villiers's words. Fayot and his wife exchange cautious glances. Only Belin, sensing an opportunity to amuse himself at little cost, leans toward Villiers with an almost unhealthy, feverish anticipation.

"Come on, Villiers, don't make us beg. What have you planned for us? It's about your cook, isn't it?"

It's true that last week the Ibo Ti Marcel, the cook on the Villiers plantation, was accused of having poisoned seven Negroes, three Negresses, two mulattoes, and one white man, Fortier the tailor.

"But do you have proof?" Déracine asks awkwardly, before Villiers's impatient and irritated eyebrows cross, silencing him.

"I promise you a first-rate show," Villiers repeats, as if Déracine hadn't said a word.

"Believe me, after seeing this, I doubt a slave will still want to poison anyone."

Then he turns to Déracine. "You want proof? Tomorrow, I'll have a confession from the accused man himself. I need witnesses to act. I invite you all. You above all, dear Déracine, because you're so worried about the legality of it all."

I record the words that immediately evoke the torture planned for Ti Marcel. Villiers rejected Belin's suggestion to have Ti Marcel whipped until blood flows.

"That torture is all too common. In my opinion they've used it so much it's no longer effective."

"Belin's idea isn't bad, though, because it would mean you wouldn't lose a Negro," Fayot reasons, always concerned with the profitability of an investment, even when it's not his own.

"I have in mind something more original, my dear friend."

All heads tilt in anticipation toward Villiers, even those belonging to the Déracines. They raise their glasses with even more liveliness, more vigor, as their bodies push against the backs of their chairs with satisfaction. The planning of torture becomes an exciting game, and not a single one of them seems to connect it to the fact that a man's life hangs in the balance.

The last time I saw Ti Marcel, he was running as usual to visit his mistress, Tontine, an Ibo woman who is the Fontaine plantation's washerwoman. The lovers would agree to meet midway between the two plantations. Fontilus and I would often tease Ti Marcel when he passed by us with a spring in his step that made him taller than he actually was. Fontilus never missed the chance to yell, "Tonton, Tontine," and Ti Marcel would wave his arm at us without stopping. Villiers's voice chases away the memory of this happy little bird with enormous wings.

The mistress's legs are crossed, as when she's had too much to drink and places an insistent hand on the thighs of the men sitting next to her. Déracine's wife wiggles like a mouse delighted to be eaten by the cat. Captivated, the men empty one glass after another without realizing it. I continue serving them with steady hands, though inside I am seeing once more the woman who was quartered on the Chatelin plantation. With each stroke the executioner had lifted scraps of flesh, digging furrows of pain through her skin. For a long time my dreams were imprisoned by the image of her shredded back. But according to Villiers, that torture was too mild, befitting only minor infractions. This was a crime of poisoning, and the punishment had to fit the crime.

"It's only an accusation," Déracine reminds them.

"We'll see tomorrow," Villiers decides, and he begins to describe the sanction he's planned. Their faces all light up to savor the long anticipated details of the torture. "Laths of red-hot iron will be applied to the soles of Ti Marcel's feet, then to his ankles and tops of his feet. Of course, with each passing hour the overseer will have to reheat the laths to 'keep his feet warm.'"

Happy with his wordplay, Villiers claims to have once seen a Negro who still couldn't place his feet on the ground six months after being tortured in this fashion.

"If Ti Marcel does not confess, my friends, you can believe he's not guilty!"

The voices of the masters reach me through a hazardous fog, and I try to not show the turmoil that's overcoming me. Out of the corner of my eye I see Jeannine, more and more at ease in her role as the new cocotte, leaning over the mistress, who has beckoned her with a gesture of her hand. Their heads, complicit and mischievous, draw close. From the small closet the cocotte brings almond sweets, which she places in the mistress's mouth with a smile. Men's words don't interest them in the least, as they mock the wrathful looks Madame Déracine sends their way and ignore me entirely. I lack the courage to continue listening to the details of the punishment reserved for Ti Marcel. My memory holds a sufficient reserve of horrors to feed my nightmares.

I am seized by the crushing truth that I am nothing but an object at the mercy of whites, while Mariette and I clear the table, serve coffee, and pass cigars to the men, which the master takes out on evenings when there are guests. The two wives have settled in a corner of the living room, where the mistress enjoys shocking her guest by lightly stroking Jeannine's chest, hair, and bare arms, all with a feigned air of innocence.

As usual, the men's conversation begins with all the complaints the planters have against the mother country. This time its refusal to trade directly with the English and Dutch prevails over all other topics. The colonists are furious because this authorization would have allowed them to make a bigger profit from syrup and molasses. Normally, these by-products are used to make tafia, but selling them would bring in higher profits. The discussion heats up while the mistress grows ever more languid, and Madame Déracine pretends to Madame Fayot not to notice a thing, all the while casting panic-stricken glances at her husband. Fayot is the most indignant of all at what he calls "a flagrant lack of liberty." Mechanically, I listen to what they say so I can think about it later, if necessary. Michaud has often told me, "Don't sniff at the information they give us—you never know when it'll come in handy." So I listen to the whites' words, but deep inside me one single idea penetrates the fog: we are at their mercy.

They can burn us slowly, blaze us like a torch, and make us shake like a kettle. They have the power. We're at their mercy, and nothing will change unless we do something. The thought severs my mind like the blow of a machete to the back of a hand. Gracieuse's ironic smile fills me with a sweet light: "Finally, little one! You've taken the time to learn the truth."

My head suddenly swarms with teeming ants. I can no longer stand to listen to them and watch them without reacting. An inevitable urgency fills me, and I feel its roar, without being able to identify it clearly—until the next day, at the edge of morning, when it surges forth of its own strength.

"Ma Augustine, tell me the story of my great-aunt Brigitte."

With clouded eyes and lips open in protestation as usual, my godmother raises her head. My voice echoes with a thousand aches that have marked our lives; my eyes are riven like a tree whose bark is cracking open. Ma Augustine feels the time for asking long-held, heartrending questions is over, and now the need to get answers brings only the smell of flowing blood. She heaves a deep sigh; she knows the time has come to hold on tight to our pain, even if the embrace tears us apart.

I have been taking out Aunt Brigitte's cord from its hiding place more and more since Fontilus's suicide, and my godmother looks now at the length of rope without touching it. Ma Augustine holds back the warning I see reflected in her eyes. Between my fingers I worry the knots, as if the cord were a long rosary of hidden regrets.

"She always wore this cord around her waist. We never knew why. She would wash it and put it on again as soon as it dried, as if it were an indispensable talisman."

I suddenly feel cold, and anguish makes me weak. I've lived my whole life honoring my aunt, cherishing everything that brought me close to her, the many traits I was said to have inherited from her: my waist, the almond shape of my eyes, the way I walk, and even my laugh. I don't want to end up with a ruined image floating in my head. Does Ma Augustine sense my apprehension? In her gentle way she caresses my cheek.

"I want so much for you to understand, Lisette. I don't want you to condemn her. She would have never hurt you or your mother. I'm sure of it, and your grandmother Charlotte, her sister, knew it as well."

Wanting to reassure me, Ma Augustine adds a small detail, like a vague aside: "You look so much like her."

It's not her fault if this refrain, repeated throughout my childhood and adolescence, doesn't rouse in me the usual bursts of pride and nostalgia for this aunt I didn't know. Instead, I feel flashes of suspicion and mistrust.

Ma Augustine begins her story calmly, as if she had long rehearsed every word, every silent pause.

"That colonist Montreuil was an arrogant and particularly cruel man, and he loved women. He was immediately attracted to Brigitte. It was clear that he only wanted her, but your aunt's wild eyes undoubtedly led him to imagine the difficulty he would have if he tried to separate us from her. Furthermore, Montreuil, wanting to get rich quickly, was thinking all the time of going into the indigo trade. He received a special price for the three of us and bought us all: Charlotte; your mother, Ayouba, still a child; and me. But he never hid his interest in your great-aunt."

"Don't forget that I was still young at that time," Ma Augustine continues. "Brigitte and Charlotte always had the instinct to protect Ayouba and me. Some things I only learned later, when my grandmother decided I was old enough to understand. And there are some details I never came to know. We were in the big house, and often Montreuil would summon Brigitte. At first she found excuses not to go to him immediately. Montreuil was a little like Fayot, only younger, bigger, and less interested in projecting the image of a rich and educated planter, and with no political ambition. He believed in pleasures one could take with the touch of a hand, without having to wait.

"In order to make Brigitte obey, he didn't hesitate to manipulate her love for her niece, Ayouba, your mother. Twice, when Brigitte refused his overtures, he had the little girl whipped. The third time he was going to have her whipped, Brigitte stopped him and followed him. On that day I think Montreuil saw the threat of death in your great-aunt's eyes. He warned her that if anything happened to him, she would be executed summarily, along with her family, which meant Charlotte, Ayouba, and me. It was without a doubt this warning that spared his life. Yet don't think that he succeeded in taming Brigitte. In fact, he was afraid of her because she knew the secrets of herbs, plants, and the human body. She could heal, but she could also injure. Montreuil knew it, but he couldn't do without her.

"This went on for years. During that time other younger, less rebellious Negresses came along, but they couldn't keep him for more than a week. Montreuil always returned, angrily looking for Brigitte like a barking dog trying to hide its hunger. The planter's wife hated Brigitte, but she was afraid of her husband. Once, when he was away, she was so bold as to have Brigitte whipped stark naked in front of the big house. When he returned, Montreuil slapped his wife before the house slaves. It seems that at your great-aunt's request, he no longer visited his wife's bed . . .

"I don't know whether this was true. Brigitte and Montreuil's story fascinated the slaves in the big house and even those in the workrooms. So they invented all sorts of rumors. Of course, they never said anything in front of Charlotte; she wouldn't have put up with it."

It's as if my grandmother is there with us in the shack. I see her stern face again as she confronts my stream of questions, but her face is filled with the gruff tenderness I knew was always there. I let myself slide down to Ma Augustine's feet and place my head on her knees. I've never felt so close to all of these women who nurtured my childhood. Their presence comforts me. Ma Augustine sits there, pensive like me, before returning to the story. I respect her silence, knowing that from now on my great-aunt's story is part of my life, never to leave.

Ma Augustine picks up where she left off. "Brigitte was the midwife for the whole region. Her reputation as healer brought dozens of women to her who suffered during the painful times of the month. White people also went to see her for a variety of ills, from simple indigestion to rheumatism. Brigitte tended to the tortured slaves whose bodies were nothing but open wounds. She relieved pains and agony, never refusing to help anyone, never asking for or accepting payment in any form. The slaves trusted her, so no one would have suspected her activities, had she not given herself up."

Ma Augustine leans toward me, and I see her staring in sadness and horror at the cord I hold between my fingers. All my anguish returns to me, like hot sweat but without a fever or chills. I too contemplate this object I've looked at so many times. What will it reveal to me about this great-aunt whom I loved even before hearing her story and whom I love a little more already even before reaching its end?

"She would always wear it around her waist. The knots got longer with the passage of the weeks, months, and years. Charlotte told me that your mother, Ayouba, asked Brigitte one day what it was. Her aunt answered, 'It's both my mercy and my hell.'

"Brigitte loved your mother. When they were together,

she would become herself again, and we caught glimpses of the Brigitte we knew before our capture, before *The Infamous Rosalie*. Talking with Ayouba, your great-aunt would rediscover her voice—a voice filled with vast spaces and malicious moons, complicit suns and fierce rains. She would rock her with stories of colors that did not exist and smells from the savannah. Ayouba would then fall asleep against her with a look of contentment on her face that she only showed when she was sleeping. Years later, when your mother got pregnant, Brigitte took care of her from the very beginning. But as the months passed, your great-aunt became increasingly irritated and nervous. When your mother reached her seventh month, Charlotte confided in me that Brigitte had ordered her to take your mother, taking me along as well. 'Charlotte, you have to get far away from here with your daughter and Augustine. I can't keep doing my work,' she had told her. Your grandmother didn't understand a word Brigitte had uttered. She thought her sister's mind had started to fail prematurely. Brigitte then pulled out the cord she sometimes hid inside her apron. 'Do you see these knots? Do you want me to add your grandchild to this cord?'"

One by one Ma Augustine's tears fall on my back. I feel them soak through the blouse's fine fabric and penetrate the shawl covering my shoulder.

The first light of dawn is beginning to fall on the fence around the shack, reminding us that soon it will be time for us to return to the big house. As if defying her instincts, my godmother leans over and touches Brigitte's cord, still clenched in my fist, with trembling hands; our hands meet and clasp above the knots frayed from the passage of time, from sun and rain. Our breaths vacillate, enveloped in tenderness before facing the words to come.

"You must understand what kind of woman your great-aunt Brigitte was. Salt of the earth, proud and generous, solid and tough like a *mapou*. Brigitte smelled of fresh herbs, of the wild and enduring smell of the forest. She was created to be free. Yes, I know the chains weigh heavy on our legs, whether man, woman, or child, whether Arada, Ibo, or Creole. I know it: I have seen so many different men and women born and die all around me. But for some, freedom and life have great gusts in common; it's the same rain, the same thunder. Brigitte and Storm, your father, were both like that. Thinking about it now, Charlotte and I, who knew her, should have suspected that she would not have accepted her status as a slave washerwoman on the Montreuil plantation without doing something about it."

"What was it that she did, Ma Augustine?"

Could that be my voice, sounding like a trickle of anguish, a rush of chaotic pulses?

"Brigitte got us to leave the plantation. I don't know what deal she struck with Villiers or whether she was helped by the slaves plotting rebellion she'd come to know. Your great-aunt didn't tell us about all her activities. Two days after we left, your great-aunt handed herself in to the constabulary."

I would have wanted to be able to stop Ma Augustine and remain wrapped in my protective silence and ignorance. But it's too late, for my life is bound to the past.

"Brigitte explained that she had killed seventy babies. At their birth she inserted a pin through the soft spot in their skull. They died from trismus soon after. No one suspected the midwife, who was always ready to lend a hand."

"She never regretted what she did. Charitable was the one who relayed her last words. She declared to the judges that it was her duty as a Negress free of mind and soul to release 'these young creatures from this shameful condition called slavery.' When they asked her why she had decided not to keep on doing so, she replied: 'Since I don't have the courage to do it for my own blood, I can no longer do it for others. I've already chased from my own body three times a baby who only would have shared my humiliation had I given birth, but I couldn't risk making my niece cry. The cord is no longer in my possession, but I can promise you that it has seventy knots, one for each baby that I saved from slavery. Today my work is finished. Do with me as you will.'"

Having lived for so long waiting with an almost painful dread for my great-aunt Brigitte's story, I now felt drained of all hope, as after the evenings of calendas, when our memories of the last dance are no longer enough to suspend our feeling of defeat and weariness that accompany our impression that nothing had changed: we remain and still are slaves. The truth of our reality dispels the fog of sensations and illusory colors with a brutal force.

Fortunately, I am too busy to let myself sink into the apathy that seized me after Vincent's leg was cut off. In the big house I wipe, wash, and tidy up. Then afterward, the messages from Michaud send me running from plantation to plantation. I slip behind the shacks to deliver them, without thinking too much, without thinking about tomorrow or about my great-aunt Brigitte—and especially without thinking about the baby growing inside me, awaiting its fate.

I take note of the comings and goings of the masters and

relate everything faithfully to Michaud. More and more slaves are visiting the one-armed man's shed, which brings an atmosphere of revolt that thrills me. On two occasions I met Maroons who gave me news of Vincent. It seems that he's near Léogâne, more determined than ever to remain a free man. He's thinking of moving toward the border and making contact with groups of Maroons who've been organizing in the eastern part of the island. My boundless love will never know any limits, except for its insatiable need for freedom. When I think of Vincent, my memories fill me, first with tender warmth, then with a faint melancholy that surprises me with the painful shivers it provokes.

My restraint, born of doubts and confusion, distances me from the other slaves in the big house. My ever-deepening involvement with Michaud and the slaves plotting rebellion makes me more cautious. When I'm with Ma Augustine, I chase all hints of uncertainty from my face. In fact, as I see her grow weaker and weaker, my thoughts turn toward nameless threats. And she hides from me the instinctual worry that takes hold of her when I'm in danger. She turns her worried look away from me before I can even question or reassure her. So we speak slowly to each other to prolong the sweetness of the present moment.

Sometimes on Sundays at Michaud's, I join other slaves who seem to be doing the same work I am. Our small group has come to gather in this yard smelling of orange trees, where the Maroon Zamor told us of Makandal's death. How long ago that seems already! So many things have happened since.

The cord has never left my body since that morning when Ma Augustine—very worried about the effects of her story on me—told me Brigitte's story. Sometimes when I feel the braided bloody knots caressing my thighs under my skirt, I shudder, because I still hear the echo of Louise's despair as she cries over her pink baby with its pink cheeks and light eyes and all those voices lamenting a lost child. I feel the weight of little Mariette's sobbing body. To feel these fibers, softened by the passage of time, against my skin is a reminder of the blood my great-aunt spilled. Seventy lives that would not come into being because she decided against it, seventy human beings who will not have the chance to see the sun rise or experience the feeling of a breeze blowing against their bare legs. But when faced with these seventy lives that will never be anything but murmurs of farewells and distress, I can't help but see again Samuel's twisted features as he lay on his deathbed, Gracieuse's inert hand, and my friend's feet, always clean in the calendas, that will never dance again. Is it preferable to die at ten years old than at birth? Will I be so reckless as to judge slaves who have claimed the right to look at themselves in the river's water without stumbling in shame?

As a well-trained domestic on the Fayot plantation who is probably worth thousands of pounds, I supervise the work of two young slaves, and the masters' visitors are impressed by my good manners. I bow my head when I am given orders, and sometimes I dodge slaps and ignore insults. Yet inside me big and unruly movements go unbridled. The memory of the barracoons come back to me with their indignant stench. I make the passage on *The Infamous Rosalie*; I feel the lashes of the whip and the wounds on my back. My skin bears the brandings and burns; my memory tells stories tinged with revolt and despair. Will I have the courage to soar above the barracoons and hold onto the stars?

Everything in me scatters and reassembles at the whim of my outbursts and dread. I am a prisoner of a past I haven't lived and am helpless as I face the coming days, which await my courage. I don't dare to face my fears.

How many days did I remain in this state of unspeakable anguish? Ma Augustine's sleepy and compassionate voice frees me when one night she murmurs in my hair: "Don't worry about me, my Lisette. I won't be in this hell much longer."

A profound calm suddenly settles deep inside me, a feeling of fullness and infinite tenderness for this gray-haired woman whose tired body is lying behind mine. How did she guess what I didn't dare to admit to myself? I pretend not to have heard, for I don't have the courage to accept the prospect of Ma Augustine's death. I don't have the heart to imagine leaving her, as she approaches the great departure.

I cry silently, aware of the emptiness that awaits me. For Ma Augustine is truly the last connection to the past that shaped me, as well as Grandma Charlotte and all the people I knew through their words in the time of the barracoons and deep in the ship's hold. Her absence will be the cruelest one.

I can already foresee how grief will overwhelm me, where exactly it will catch my heart and twist it mercilessly: when the smell of ginger and verbena reaches me, filled with our moments of shared silence; when I no longer feel the weight of her tenderness on my longing locks; when I look in vain for her frail and proud figure at the crossroads of a path.

How many dawns will I see before I accept that I've forever lost her from sight?

Michaud understands that my mind is made up. He also seems to know instinctively that I need time and space.

"I'm taking care of everything, Lisette."

Suspended between my current status as house slave and Maroon-in-training, I look with calm eyes on everything around me. Ma Augustine is not mistaken; her every gesture bids me farewell. She sinks into a fog that I can't penetrate. I unsettle her with questions steeped in the scent of rain, with fits of ambiguous, sad laughter. I engage her with heartbreaking smiles, with a tenderness that flows from every corner of our shared grief.

"Let me go in peace, my girl," she finally tells me.

As surely as the sun rises in the morning on these hills, I know for certain that after I leave, my godmother will soon let herself die. I will not be by her side, and someone else's hand will close her eyelids.

I won't see her again.

So I take her hand and place it on my belly, on this child I've just decided to keep. Only now. Maybe because I've just understood that I owe the woman I am to these two women who were willing to live under slavery in large part for my sake. They've accompanied me on my path until I can stand and face the barracoons.

"The slaves on the Lalanne plantation have risen," Michaud tells me when I see him again, two days later, while in me dwells my wild and desperate desire to give birth to this baby I don't know yet but whom I want to be as fearless and proud as its father.

Michaud's voice cuts like a blade of steel. Danger threatens us.

"Some rebels managed to escape to the hills after burning the refinery and killing the overseer and manager, but two slaves seem to have been arrested from the plantation. Apparently, a slave from the big house accused them. Whites in the region are on guard, Lisette. I'm sure that there's also a spy among the slaves at Fayot's. I have my suspicions, but I don't like to accuse anyone without proof. Be careful. You have to leave earlier than expected. I've arranged everything for tomorrow morning at dawn."

That night, drawn by the uneasiness that had been haunting me for a while, I head toward the shack Clarisse and her daughter share with Rose-Marie. By the light of the flickering candle, through the half-open door, I glimpse Rose-Marie's profile and little Joséphine sitting at her feet. A slight tug in my heart reminds me of all the times I've sat at the feet of Grandma Charlotte and Ma Augustine. Tears fill my eyes, but I wipe them away angrily. It's no time for tears or complaints. Out of habit I weave my way toward the big house, without really seeing where I'm going, since the moonlight doesn't penetrate the trees' foliage. Once inside, I move silently toward the master's room, instinctively adopting the furtive step I will assume for my survival. At the end of the corridor I catch a glimpse of Fayot's shadow leaning to hear Clarisse, whose voice I recognize. Their suspicious attitude reinforces my own. Though I can only make out the quadroon's words with great difficulty, I hear her say my name and Michaud's. That's enough for me. I don't linger any longer, leaving the big house as stealthily as I entered it. My first instinct is to run to warn my one-armed confidant, then a rage so enormous it frightens me, and I change my mind . . .

Here I am on the road heading west.

A Maroon.

Without shelter, without masters or mistresses, we walk in a straight line, each lost in her own thoughts and regrets, in her own farewells and dreams of freedom. Do we have the right to sacrifice our companions in misery in order to be free? Last night I waited for Clarisse to leave the big house, and then confronted her with my accusations. The quadroon's laugh sprung like twigs of firewood with an insolence that stoked my anger.

"I have nothing against you, Lisette. Listen carefully: I don't want to wait six or seven years to be freed. That bastard Malary didn't hesitate to abandon me and his daughter, though he had promised to free us both. Joséphine has to get out from under Fayot's wife's control at all costs. You see how Madame hates Joséphine. I want the other children I bear to be free. I have nothing against you, but Fayot promised to free us this year, me and Joséphine, if I give him the names of the slaves who are conspiring against him. That's all."

On the wide road heading west, I picture once more the horror on Clarisse's face as she realizes I'm going to hurt her. By the time I realized it myself, my hands were already around her neck.

"It seems that Arada women are made for love," Fontilus told me one day. "With a bottom like yours, you could birth ten babies as big and beautiful as you."

Last night my strength helped me to subdue Clarisse,

stifle her screams, and drag her body all the way to the back of the storehouse, where I hid it. Then I went and told Rose-Marie to warn Michaud to run for cover. The former overseer with the vengeful arm will have to join the Maroons, but I'm not surprised he decided to stay a little longer.

"If I leave the area now, I'll cause a lot of trouble for everyone who uses me as a contact. To tell the truth, I don't feel like moving from here. Don't worry about me. I'll know how to get by." One more farewell. Yet another absence that can never be replaced.

On the road heading west, on jagged paths through hills and forests.

A thousand fleeting sensations to feel, a thousand images disappearing at our steps' persistence, under the rising sun. I cling desperately to the smells of all the shacks, to the scent of ginger, to the panic-filled taste of my tears, to the heartbreaking touch of my godmother's dress against my cheek. Ma Augustine wasn't sleeping last night when I came in her shack after talking to Rose-Marie. She was waiting, sitting on the old straw chair, our blanket riddled with holes over her legs. She looked so vulnerable to me as she faced the looming sorrow that the tears I'd held back for so long sprung forth. As her body reaches the end of its journey, I let her see my weakness, just as when Samuel would pull my braids, and I fled with scratched legs in search of my portion of tenderness among the folds of Grandma Charlotte and Ma Augustine's skirts.

I cried like I surely will never cry again.

Ma Augustine hardly uttered a word when I told her I was about to leave, as if our last moments together were not particularly important, as if it was just another moment we were sharing, fragile, particular, and everlasting, like all the others. Except that when I finished shedding my tears, she caressed my belly with a still-hesitant gesture and smiled— she whose smiles life had stolen long ago.

"It will be a girl, Lisette."

So I let myself be carried along on this surge of tenderness, and I wanted for one last time to curl up into her protective embrace as I would when I was a child. "She will be an Arada girl like Aunt Brigitte, like Grandma Charlotte, like my mother, like you, Ma Augustine."

And I added, with just the slightest hesitation in my already hoarse voice, "An Arada woman like me."

Ma Augustine responded in a voice laden with suffering too true to ever be forgotten. "A Creole like you, Lisette."

Then a glint of hope filled her eyes, more luminous than a moon's ray trembling near the clouds, and she added this wish, which came my way like a new talisman: "May this country be hers one day!"

On the wide road heading west, I take in the tenacious smell of life found in the stones scratching my skin, in the touch of the sun brushing me. I stop to take a breath. Around us are the hills, a solid, familiar landscape. They have chased away the mist of dawn and seem to defy me. I hold a single truth: the promise I make to the small being inside me, in the name of everyone who has helped me retrace my steps since the night of the barracoons, everyone who took me by the hand to teach me about the steerage of *The Infamous Rosalie* and the thousand roundabout paths shame can take, everyone who showed me the many milky ways where my need for dignity could soar. It's my turn now to walk with my daughter, who will be born, like me, from this land of waves and mountains and whose fate is anchored in the four corners of this island.

Aunt Brigitte's cord, riding against my belly, reminds me of the promise of love and dignity I made in her honor as well. I must wrap myself in passion and light so I don't fear the emptiness and so I can teach my daughter to confront the barracoons and soar to the stars.

Most of all, my love for her must be as wide as the blue sky and sea. May I find the courage to honor my promise: Creole child who still lives in me, you will be born free and rebellious, or you will not be born at all.

Afterword

I wasn't intending to write a historical novel. Two years ago, when I was reading one day, I came upon an incident recounted in *La Révolution aux Caraïbes.** Captivated by the story of an Arada midwife, I wrote a short story based on her experience, then I placed both in the back of a drawer and the back of my mind.

Later, as if she had only retreated in order to strengthen her grip on me, the Arada midwife returned to haunt me with quiet resolution. So I immersed myself in the historical time of the great fear of poisoning on the island of Saint-Domingue and all the excesses it brought out in the relationships between human beings as well as the tragedies and horrors, atrocities and indignities, that define the institution of slavery. I attempted as best I could to respect the historical context. But I admit that what was most essential for me was to imagine and create men, women, and

---

* M. E. Descourtilz cites the case of an Arada midwife who, during her trial, revealed a necklace made of rope that she wore in which each knot represented one of the seventy children she had killed: "To remove these young creatures from the shameful institution of slavery, I inserted a needle in their brain through the fontanel at the moment of their birth. The result was trismus, so deadly on the island, and whose cause you now know" (qtd. in *Antilles 1789: La Révolution aux Caraïbes*, ed. L. Abenon, J. Cauna, and L. Chauleau [Paris: Éditions Nathan, 1989], 77).

children living through this infamy filled with complex emotions and passions.

I wasn't intending to write a historical novel. May I be forgiven, then, for the few discrepancies and creative liberties I've taken. I only seek to acknowledge my characters' humanity. Yet I must refuse any responsibility for the torture and punishment described in the text. They are all unfortunately true, born of the cruel and perfidious imagination of those who proclaimed themselves to be civilized.